Layin' It Bare

LOVÉ

Simple Pleasures Publishing

Simple Pleasures Publishing

ISBN: 978-0-578-26074-7

PRINTED IN THE UNITED STATES OF AMERICA

CONTENTS

EVERYDAY PEOPLE

*T*he definition of a family varies from person to person. The basis of most is that a family is a group of persons sharing common ancestry. You would think that a family is supposed to be supportive and stick together. On the other hand, there are many who like to keep shit going with gossip, back biting, and lies. Much of the family breakdown comes from each other worrying about the wrong things instead of addressing the right ones. They would rather talk about who is sleeping with whom, who is drinking too much, or even how much money someone makes and how they spend it. These are all things that could remain unsaid and be considered personal business, but there are also things that just need to be laid bare.

Every family has secrets and some should stay as such. The Andersons weren't an exception.

Angelia Anderson, or Angie, was known as the

family shit starter. Every time there was some type of mess going in their family please believe that Angie was in the middle of it. Despite how tight-lipped she was about what was going on in her own home, she made it her business to know what was going in everyone else's. Most of the family didn't want to be bothered with Angie, and they only interacted with her when they had to. Angie had pretty much been exiled into her own universe because of the situation between her man and her niece. Nothing could be said or done that would change what was going to happen.

Angie had a jealous heart and everyone knew it. Every now and again she would zone out and start staring at people. She would analyze a person from head to toe and later when slightly provoked she would pick them apart. She tried to hide her shortcomings with snide remarks and cruel jokes. Humor was the way she dealt with her issues. But, one of her major issues was that she could not take the same things she dished out. What she found funny, others found offensive. The old saying about criticizing others to make yourself feel good was a true testament for her.

Angie had a bad case of low self-esteem; she had been hiding from herself for years. Most of her weight used to be in her breast, they were a size 42HH. But after she had a breast reduction, it looked like all that weight shifted to her belly which seemed to have split into two. When she stood up straight, it looked like she had two stomachs. She also hated the fact that she didn't have much booty; her sister Chell got all of that. Both of these issues caused her to always wear shirts that were 2-3 sizes too big for her. There were no full length mirrors in her home because she didn't want to look at her body, not even by accident. The one thing that Angie did have was a pretty face. She always kept her hair and toes on point. Angie didn't bother with her fingernails because of the chemicals of her trade as a hairdresser, but once in a while she would get some tips put on for special occasions. She would always say "I may not be a size 10 but I will look like one from the neck up."

Doctors have suggested that she lose weight, but that only made her eat more. As with many overweight people, food was used to fill a void. Whenever she was upset, depressed, or angry, she ate which only caused those same symptoms to be repeated. And because of her attitude everyone was too scared to say anything to her.

It was hard to understand why she let Earl get away with murder but anybody else had to walk on eggshells. Her tongue could cut like a razor and it didn't matter who she was talking to either. If Angie didn't like what they were doing or saying, she would step in with her two cents. On the other hand she could be really fun to be around. Angie did have a good heart in there somewhere. On rare occasions she would let it show and would go out of her way to help others in need. But this was a trick because this is how she drew people in only to eventually set them up for failure. But once the honeymoon phase was over and you got to know her there were not many kind words from her lips. And on the rare occasion that she did say something pleasant, you better believe that behind your back the horns will come out. Angie was miserable and she made sure that everyone she dealt with felt the same. This caused many arguments and broke up many friendships and family relations.

BABY I'M A STAR

I didn't come from a good family; I pretty much raised myself. My mama was unlucky with men and had 14 kids with 4 different men; I was in the first set. Mama took care of all 14 of us in a 3 bedroom shack. To say that we didn't have much would be an understatement. We didn't have shit! Mom relied on men to take care of her, and they did, problem was she kept spitting out babies. When it was too many of us, the fellas didn't come by so often. It was four of us in my set and since we were all boys, we had to drop out of school to make money for the family. Mama didn't care if we went to school or not; making money was more important. We didn't care either because wasn't any of us going to be rocket scientists. So when each of us made it to the 9th grade, we dropped out and went to work. When we got paid, she took all of our money. She didn't give us nothing outta our checks but $20! Mama used to say we were too stupid to know what to do with money. One day my older brother Nate got so fed up with her taking our hard-earned cash and using it to take care of her no-count niggas that he just up and hauled ass one night and never came back. Mama found out that he had been saving his $20 until he had enough money to make a run for it. Mama was mad as shit after that so then we only got a few bucks every once in a while. It didn't take long for the rest of us to follow Nate's lead and get the hell on, too.

Life was hard for me in the beginning. I was an uneducated black man on my own in the deep south. I had to teach myself about life and find my own way day by day. I lived in the small town of Maplesville, AL, not too far from where I grew up. The only decent place to work in town was at the local race track. It paid ok, but there were only so many jobs available so I had to learn how to hustle. Sure, I've had my ups and downs in the game, but now things have turned out better than I could have ever imagined.

Today I got it good. I got money in my pocket, my ol' lady worships the ground I walk on, and I got a few chicks on the side. Shit, I don't have to lift a finger around here. My girl Angie makes sure that I have everything I think I want, and half the time I don't even have to ask. Angie has had my back from day one. She has always been there for me when I needed it the most. She always put me first, and that is just how I like it. Angie was a pretty girl, but she was a big girl with low self esteem. Angie's issues made it easy for me to manipulate her because all she wanted was for someone to pay attention and love her. So I did that. In the beginning, I took the time to spoil her with what I could. I didn't have much money, but what I had, I gave to her freely. I treated her like she was the moon and the stars to me. Angie ate it up just like I knew she would. I had got so good up in her head that I knew what she wanted before she knew it.

For the past five years Angie was my woman. She came along at a time in my life when I needed someone to hold me down. I had just got out of jail from a three-year stint and had no one and nowhere to go. My family couldn't help because they were struggling too. Then my lucky ass I ran into Angie at a camp stew meeting. They weren't really meetings; they were more like get-togethers where the locals would grill out, drink, play cards or bones, and see who made the best camp stew. That night Angie won for the best stew. I didn't recognize her at first, but once she came over to say hi, it clicked.

I was actually dating Angie's sister, Michelle, when we first met. Let me tell you that girl was fine as hell; Chell had a body like a coke bottle and the sweetest lovin' I ever had. When we hooked up, she was a wild one. We were both in our early 20's at the time, but Chell already had a kid. We would party all night, smoke weed, and drink. But that wasn't enough for her; she eventually graduated to cocaine. In the beginning it was just once in a while, and I didn't mind that because she was my woman. I had been in the game for a while by then, and I knew that I would be able to control her dope habit because she was getting it from me. I also knew that once the dope got 'em, you can never trust 'em again. With women you have to have some type of hold over them, and for Chell, coke was her hold. Boy did I love me some Chell. After a while, we started having some problems because she had started using coke too heavily. I couldn't control her. Plus, she started stealing my shit. Then when things got back on track with us, I got busted.

While I was locked up, Chell went back home to Bolingbrook, Illinois, to get herself clean. From what I heard, she went back and forth to rehab for a few years before she succeeded. During that time, she had 2 more kids, who had to live with other family members until she got her self straight. Once she was clean, I knew that she would never come back to me. When I tried to holla at her, she told me that I was part of the bad habit she had to kick, and that was that. Now she's married and doing better than I ever expected. So when I ran into Angie, we just started kicking it. She knew about my past with Chell and didn't care. Within a few months of dating, she let me move in with her. After about 2 years of living in the projects, I bought us one of them nice doublewide trailer homes and some land in my old neighborhood, and we've been there ever since.

Things were pretty good between Angie and me. I even tried to go legit and started my own landscaping business. Things were slow in the beginning because I was new. The bills still needed to get paid so I had to do something extra. With no real money coming in, I had to go back to what I knew-- hustling. I kept my business going and slowly built up my clientele. After a while, my lawn business picked up, but I kept my hustle on the side because the money was good. I used to try and hide my hustle from Angie because I was afraid that it would scare her off because she was a church going woman. She, unlike her sister, was not in the game. My gal was a good one. She kept the house clean, cooked my food, bought my clothes, and sexed me any way I wanted without any questions. I lucked out and got me a good, honest Christian woman, or so I thought.

One time I slipped up and let her find a case full of money that I was hiding, and that's when the shit hit the fan. I tried to lie, but the heifer saw straight through me. I came home one day and the house was quiet. I should have known then that something was up.

"Where the hell you been?" Angie barked.

"Who you talking to like that woman?" I asked shocked as shit because Angie never talked to me like that, being a Christian and all.

"I'm talking to yo simple ass. Where did all this money come from?" Angie asked holding my stash.

"I…uh…I've been working more yards."

"That is a lie because you don't make money like this fixing yards."

I went to snatch my case and was surprised when she snatched it back. Like I said, Angie was a big girl, at least 275. I only weighted 160, so she had the advantage.

"I know you been out hustling and I was just waiting to catch you. Oh yeah, I also know about that bitch over in the old projects that you been messin' wit. All this time I've been taking care of your sorry ass, not once did you offer me a dime and you got the nerve to be out fucking around, too. You must think I'm a blind fool or something. I got a trick for your ass. You gonna rue the day you ever tried to get over on me, nigga."

And she wasn't lying. Ever since that day, she keeps a tight leash on me. Every time I leave the house, I have to answer a million questions, and when I get back she's always asking for money. I was tempted to leave her ass, but I couldn't because she had too much on me. She knows about Lamar. He had been taking money from me for months before I caught his thievin' ass. Let's just say that he won't take anything from nobody else. She knows about all the dope I'm slinging and where I hide my stashes. Hell, she even rode with me to Georgia on a few drops. I should've never taken her because now she knows my connects, too. So now I guess I'm kinda stuck with her. In the end, it was all good because Angie turned out to be down as hell. And the truth be told, I ain't never gonna find another woman like her to hold me down. The only problem I have with Angie is that she can act a plum fool sometimes, but as long as I give her money and let her feel like she is in control…she is happy.

To be honest, I don't know what these women see in me. I know I'm not the most handsome fella, but that shit doesn't matter these days. A nigga can be black as tar, have two rusty teeth, finger waves, no car, no house, and no real job. But as long as you got that dolla dolla bill, bitches will follow… trust me I know because that was me in a nut shell.

I know that Angie's friends, the few that she does have, may wonder why she is still with me. In the beginning, Angie was a sweetheart but now she makes a joke of cussin' and fussin' at me in front of folks all the damn time, and I just take it. My revenge is stepping out with other women. Everybody knows that I step out on her…hell, I've stepped out with some of her trifling ass friends, but that was her fault. When her home-girls would come over, Angie took joy in tormenting them. She would talk about their big asses, tits, and who they were sleeping with. She would even go as far as to raise up their skirts and tell me to look at their drawers. Once in a while, one would look back at me just to see if I was looking. That was my cue.

Her friends may think that I've changed her for the worst, but what they don't know is that Angie has always been as bad as me. Angie is a street hustling kitchen beautician. She was good and cheap just like they liked it. We always have women coming in and out of the house getting their hair fixed, gossiping, buying and selling shit. I never questioned her about how she paid the bills and bought me stuff just as long as she wasn't bothering me. Come to find out Angie wasn't as innocent as she came off to be. I know about her bad check writing, gambling, stealing cable, grocery store scams, and the food stamp and section eight fraud. She even got a federal charge against her for receiving stolen merchandise, which she could have avoided if she had listened to me. She went into the store with the lady, pointed out what she wanted and waited for her outside. As soon as the girl got into the truck, the poe-poe got 'em. With that shit on her record, it's been hard for her to get a real good paying job. So she sticks to doing hair and hustling on the side.

I'll admit that I have fought with Angie a time or two, but that was normal. Every now and again all that fussin' and cussin' gets old, and I just need her to shut the fuck up. Now don't get it twisted, Angie ain't nothing to play wit. I 'member this one time we went to a little hole-in-the-wall club called the Soul Inn. This club or juke joint as we used to call it was just that. Everyone in there belonged to somebody, and it was usually not the person they were there with. The space couldn't be any bigger than a gas station, but it stayed full of people. The inside was dark and crowded with make-shift furniture. Most of the tables were rickety and had to be held up by folded newspaper or books. The bar was a piece of plywood stacked on two large speakers that didn't even work. The walls were bare, and the floors were dusty. Majority of the folks hung out outside because there was no air conditioning. It was a wonder that the place did so well. I guess the cheap booze and Mattie's fried chicken were the cause for so many of us still hanging around.

Anyway, me and Angie went out to party a little bit before the last days of summer were over. I admit, it was my fault, but Angie showed her natural black ass. I went to the bar to get my set up of Paul Masson, ice, and soda and there she was in a skin tight cat suit with some of those super freak thigh-boots on. I knew her from back in the day so I smiled and spoke to her. Cynthia was as fine as frog's hair, and she knew it, too. This was the kind of girl that used what she had to get exactly what she wanted, and now that I had come up, she was trying to use that shit on me. I told her that I was wit my ol' lady but she was like "So, what's that supposed to mean?" I told her Angie didn't play that shit and that she needed to gwon-about her business, but she didn't listen. Everything was fine until things went a little too far on the dance floor. You know how people get after a few drinks… sloppy. Both of us had almost forgotten Angie was even there with me because she just sat back in the cut just watching. Throughout the night, Cynthia kept flirting with me and after a few drinks, I started flirting pack. Mistake number one.

The DJ had started playing the blues and me and baby girl were getting it in! Angie didn't mind me dancing with other women; it's just that I couldn't get too freaky on the floor. Baby girl had all the ass a man could stand, any more and you could hurt ya self. The whole mood was right. Then out of nowhere, Angie snatched me up off the girl. You know the old saying that alcohol is liquid courage; well this silly bitch must have been on full because she snatched me back. Mistake number 2.

"You better un-ass my man if you know what's good for ya," Angie yelled over the music.

"He ain't acting like he your man now, so what chu want?"

"Earl, let's go!"

"Nawl, he ain't gotta go nowhere bitch, 'cause he wit me now."

"Earl, you betta tell this bitch what time it is before I have to."

By now I was good and tipsy and really didn't know what to do. The music had stopped, and all eyes were on us. Black folk always want to see some shit go down, and then they be the first ones yelling "it couldna been me." I have to admit I was enjoying it. There ain't nothing like a woman fighting over you. Shit, they the ones who look stupid while the man look like a pimp.

"Bitch, you ain't gonna do shit. It ain't my fault you big ass can't keep your man in check," Cynthia said with that sista girl neck roll and finger pointing.

I took this as my cue to move out of the way before I get hit or something because I knew that Angie was about to pop. Cynthia stood toe to toe with Angie and put her hand in Angie's face. Mistake number 3. Next thing you know it was like that scene from *The Color Purple* when Sophia knocked Squeak into that water hole. Angie stepped back, and before Cynthia could blink, she got knocked up under the bar stools. Angie dared her to get up and finish what she had started, but Cynthia was down for the count with her right eye already starting to swell. When Angie looked at me, all I could do was hold my head down and walk out the door. As I stepped towards the car, I could hear the club erupting with laughter and the music being crunk back up. The ride home was quiet, and I knew that if I said anything, she might unleash the rest of Cynthia's ass whoppin' on me, and in my half drunken state, I wouldn't stand a chance. That was the last time I ever danced with another woman in Angie's presence.

From time to time, we would still get into it over some random chick, but we always worked it out. I know that Angie ain't ever cheated on me, and she never will. Me on the other hand, I have to have a variety. Shit, these women can't get enough of my ass. They are always sliding numbers in my pocket and all up in my face when Angie ain't around. They know I'm with Angie, but they be like, "What's that got to do with me?" What man is going to turn down some free pussy? Not me. I got this bad ass chick named Meka from the old project we stayed in that I thought I was hiding from Angie. How she found out about Meka is beyond me, but as long as she doesn't know ol' girl is pregnant with my twins, everything is cool. Besides, I don't know if they mine anyway. These bitches see how good Angie got it, and they all want to take her place. There is only one woman that can do that.

Everything is Gonna Be Alright

See me and Uncle Earl go way back. He has been there ever since I was a baby. You could say that he is my father figure, but not my father. As a baby I was bounced back and forth from Bolingbrook to Maplesville. I didn't come to live with Aunt Angie permanently until I was about six. I came to them after my mama was sent to jail on drug charges. My aunt never had any kids because of a so-called childhood "accident," so she was more than happy to take me in. In the beginning, life was good. Aunt Angie bought me everything a little girl could dream of and more. We went shopping all the time, all on Uncle Earl, and he never said a word. I used to dream about having a man just like him when I grew up.

As they say, all good things come to an end and Auntie had changed on me. My end was started a few years after I got here. It was like the older I got the more my aunt can't stand me. Sometimes I feel like she had changed my name to black ass.

"Tesha, get yo black ass in this house before I come and get you," Angie yelled through the screen door. *That girl just makes me sick, always in Earl's face. And her filling out so early hasn't helped matters any.*

"Yes ma'am," Tesha said as she slid past Angie's large frame covering the front door.

It was as if she was daring me to move her or something. I don't know why she is so mean sometimes; I'm starting to hate it here. If it weren't for Uncle Earl, I would go back to Bolingbrook.

"Tesha, I'm going out for a minute and I want you to have the living room, kitchen, and bathrooms cleaned and do the laundry," Angie demanded while gathering her purse and keys. "I need to go to the flea market, and no I don't need any company."

I need to buy Earl something to wear for Saturday. Maybe some new Tommy shirts and matching jeans-- he should like that and maybe show me some attention around here, Angie thought to herself as she exited the front door.

Tesha ran to the front window to make sure that Angie left before she went back outside to see

Earl. *I'll be damned if I'm going sit in this house and play Cinderella.*

Tesha sat next to Earl under the shade tree and asked in her sweetest voice, "Uncle Earl, do I have to clean the whole house by myself?"

"Tesha, you know how your aunt is. She just mad and need to blow off some steam. I gave her five hundred bones before she left, so she'll be alright in about six hours. I'll help you clean up, so don't worry about it. What do you want to do?"

"I don't know...can I have a sip of your drink?"

"Yeah, baby girl, you can have whatever you want from me. Go get you a cup."

So for the next two hours Tesha and Earl sat under the shade tree drinking Paul Masson and talking about life.

"So, Tesha, do you have a boyfriend?" Earl asked pouring her another drink.

"No, I don't have time for boys."

"Good. Boys only bring problems and babies, and you don't need either." You need to set your sights higher and find a man that can do something for you and not just to you, you know what I mean?

"I think so, Uncle Earl," Tesha said in an unsure voice.

"You can drop the Uncle Earl bit; it's just us out here."

"Ok…Earl."

By now the Paul she was drinking had started to make Tesha tingle and become lightheaded. She wanted to show Earl that she was a big girl who could handle her liquor, so she started pretending to drink by just letting the strong liquid touch her lips.

"Tesha, can I tell you something?" Earl asked trying to come up with the right words.

"Yeah Unc—Earl," Tesha said catching herself.

"Ya see a man has needs and most of his life, he is looking for a woman to fulfill those needs. And when he finds her, he has no problem giving her the world. Now you remember that and you can't lose."

Earl sat back and took a puff from his Newport and smiled to himself. He knew that was all he needed to say. Tesha was a bright girl; she just needed some guidance, and if she had to learn, why shouldn't he be the teacher?

"Is that what you and Aunt Angie have?" Tesha quizzed.

"Not quite. Ya see your aunt and I have a long complicated past. We started out that way, but over time things have changed. She is not there for me like she should be, and it's like now all she wants is my money. She doesn't care how she looks no more, and she does more fussing now than ever, and it is starting to get on my nerves. I need a woman who cares for me and for what I need, not just what she can get from me. You know what I mean?"

"I think so, Earl. Is that why you are having all those other women?" Tesha said not sure if she overstepped her boundary.

"Exactly. If I had that one good woman, I wouldn't need those other women. If I had a woman who liked the same things I liked, we could be real good. Take us for instance. Me and you can go hunting, fishing and shooting together like we were old friends. Those are some of the qualities I want in my woman."

"Oh, I see," Tesha said taking a real sip this time.

The wheels were turning for Tesha. She knew that Earl preferred her over Angie, and he had just confirmed her notions. Now all she had to do was prove to him that she was the better woman; then she could move on to the good life without her messy ass aunt around.

That night, Tesha dreamed of how her life would be with Earl. It was so real that she could feel it. In her slumber, she saw them living together with no worries on a nice quiet stretch of land with a pond where they could go fishing any time they want. There was no Angie and no mess from the family. They didn't even keep in contact with anyone because they just will never understand their love. It was just the two of them against the world.

All of a sudden, Tesha was awakened by some-one shouting. As soon as she rolled over to see what was going on, she knew instantly that it was her aunt and Earl fussing again. Only God knows what this argument was about this time. There had been many a night that Tesha would lay awake in her bed and listen to them go at it, and most of the time, she was the topic. She knew that her aunt didn't want her around anymore, but she also knew that Earl did, and he usually got his way when it came to what he wanted. After a few minutes of eavesdropping, Tesha realized it was nothing, so she rolled over and went back to sleep.

The morning sun greeted Tesha with a smile. Her dreams of Earl put a new purpose in her life. From this point on, she knew she had to have Earl all to herself because she could treat him better. Her mind was made up now, and she felt that no other woman could do the things she could do for him. As far as she was concerned, it was a matter of time before she was the woman in his life. Angie had her chance to be the woman he needs, but she blew it; now it's her turn to be the woman he wants. Angie could go to hell because she stopped being the loving aunt years ago. Now it was about her happiness and everyone else can kick rocks.

FAKE

"Angie, something just ain't right with those two," Betty called out from the kitchen.

"What do you mean, auntie?"

"Them two being as close as they are; that's what I mean."

"Ain't nothing going on Auntie. They're okay. Earl is just like a father to Tesha. She needs a male role model," Angie said trying not to sound too annoyed. She was not doing a good job. She felt that they were getting a little too close also.

"Don't play dumb, gal. I think he messing wit her." Now Betty was standing right in front of Angie.

"Why yawl always gotta go there? Earl ain't messin' with no Tesha, I would know!" Angie was getting madder by the second.

"Angie you mean to tell me that you alright with them always together?"

"Yeah. They just close that's all."

"Humph," Betty said sucking her teeth.

"You know what Betty, you always talking about what's going on in my family. What about what went down when I was a child, huh, nobody want to talk about that? As I recall you were there too and you didn't have much to say then but now you want to tell me how to run my house. How about you sweep around your own front door before you try to sweep around mine. I gotta go!" Angie slammed her cup down on the table and stormed out of the house.

Angie cussed and mumbled to herself all the way to the car. "All she cares about is Tesha and Earl…she didn't even tell me how cute my new hairdo was!"

Angie spoke aloud to herself once she was in the car.

I hate coming over to Betty's house. She always has her damn nose in somebody's business. Every time I turn around somebody is talking about Earl and Tesha, like they the only two alive. Besides, I have already talked to Earl about the time he spends with Tesha, and he said it's nothing.….So it's nothing.

Earl can be a good man at times and during those times he isn't, I just have to deal with it because that is part of being in a relationship. We have our ups and downs just like any other relationship; it's just that lately most of our problems revolve around Tesha. I'm trying to do the Godly thing and see after her, but every day I want to send her black ass packing.

Truth is Angie knew that Betty was on to something because as she drove, she thought back to last night. When she got home from shopping she was greeted with a surprise. Earl and Tesha were sitting on the sofa all cozy and shit....there were other seats available.

"What's going on here?" she asked closing the door behind her.

"Aagh here you go," Earl said getting up and walking toward the bedroom.

"Tesha, get in that kitchen and clean up."

"Yes ma'am," Tesha said in a nervous voice.

After Angie surveyed her surroundings and saw nothing out of place, she just pushed it out of her head and gave Tesha the food she brought home for dinner. Angie figured that she would have to carry Tesha's hot tail with her whenever she left from now on. Maybe then, her family will stop talking about what's going on in her household.

TOO CLOSE

The conversation with Aunt Betty lingered in Angie's ears for the rest of the night. She tried her best to just let the whole thing go, but it did not work. Angie could not believe the nerve of Betty to question what was going on in her house, especially with how she half-raised her daughters. Although Angie would never admit it, Aunt Betty had her thinking that having a little chat with Tesha would not hurt.

Later that evening after the kitchen had been cleaned and everyone was getting ready for bed, Earl decided to sneak out the back door. Angie saw him and thought to herself that his ass thinks he's nickel slick, but she know what was up. Humph, he's probably heading over to Meka's house. I'm just gonna take advantage of this time alone with Tesha.

"Tesha ,come in here or a minute. I wanna talk to you," Angie said walking towards her bedroom.

"Yes ma'am." Not knowing where this was going, Tesha decided to just be honest because she knew Angie could always tell when she was lying.

"Baby you know that you can tell your auntie anything, right?

Tesha just shook her head up and down.

"Well, I want to know if anything is happening with you that I should know about." Angie motioned for Tesha to sit next to her on the bed.

"No ma'am."

"You would tell me if it were, right?" This was more of a statement than a question.

"Yes ma'am."

"No matter what it is or who is involved I will still love you and protect you."

Tesha just sat there looking because she got scared. *Does she know about us?* She remained quiet as not to put her foot in her mouth. Earl always taught her that in unsure situations it is better to listen and watch than to talk, so that is what she did.

"You're a teenager now and you're developing into a young woman. There will be boys out there who are going to try and test you. I want you to be prepared for when that time comes. So if there is anything you want to know, now is the time to ask." Angie said this with a pat on Tesha's shoulder for extra emphasis.

"I un…I don't have anything to ask you Auntie."

"How about we start with the birds and the bees. Tell me what you know about sex."

This took Tesha completely off guard because her Auntie has never shown much interest in her until now and to use sex of all things to break the ice with.

"What about it?" Tesha asked wrenching her hands in her lap.

"Are you having it?" Angie stated

That's my auntie, straight up with no chaser.

"No!" Tesha said moving away from Angie's grip.

"Baby, don't get upset. I just want to know if anybody has been trying to do sex stuff to you, that's all. I don't want you to get hurt."

Angie saw a glimmer of sadness come across Tesha's face. She knew that she had struck a nerve.

"Baby, talk to me. Has anyone tried to touch you?" This time Angie actually sounded concerned.

Tesha just looked at the wall, she was almost trance-like. Then her lips started moving and Angie could not believe her ears.

Tesha started in a low, monotonous voice. Her mind drifted back to the first lesson Earl taught her. She told Angie selected bits and pieces of their first encounter which had occurred one day when Angie was out shopping. Earl had walked in on her in the bathroom while she was coming out of the shower. Tesha said that he just stood there looking at her as if she was an alien from another planet. She said that when she tried to cover herself he stopped her by grabbing her towel. Tesha paused and looked at the floor as if it were going to give her some answers as to what to do.

"Then what?" Angie asked getting as close to Tesha as she possibly could.

Through fresh tears, Tesha began telling Angie what happened in the simplest way possible. While in her mind, every detail of that event ran wild.

Earl rubbed her hair, then her shoulder, on down her back and stopped at her butt. She said that she began to shake from the draft and Earl told her it was okay and that he was not going to hurt her. Tesha continued to tell Angie that Earl rubbed her butt until the wetness was gone; then he turned her around to face the wall. All the while, Earl was telling Tesha how beautiful she was and that he was not going to hurt her if she just cooperated. What Tesha was leaving out was that she started to tingle inside and didn't know why. Her mind was telling her that this was not right, but her body was speaking another language. Tesha didn't know what sex was, but she knew that it was supposed to be something between a man and a woman who cared about each other. Sex was just not something that was talked about in her family. Besides, she cared about Earl and he cared about her so it was ok.

"Tesha, I want you to turn around and lay up against the wall and put your foot on the tub." Earl instructed her while he was rubbing her back side.

Tesha complied, not wanting to disappoint Earl.

"Please don't hurt me Earl," she whimpered.

"I won't, baby girl. Just trust me, okay."

"Okay," she whimpered again.

Earl knew that she was a virgin and could understand her fear.

After Tesha leaned on the wall, Earl started to rub her from the top of her ass to the bottom. Then he eased his hand down into her secret place. It was warm and he could feel her muscles contracting in apprehension. As he gently massaged her clit until he heard her breathing change, he felt her loosen up. This was a good sign to Earl, and he took it as an okay to do further.

"Do you want me to stop, Tesha?" Earl asked massaging her womanhood a little harder.

Tesha surprised herself when she shook her head no. She didn't know what he was doing to her, but she knew that it was like nothing she had ever felt before. Earl got down on his knees. She did as she was told and rested up against the bathroom wall. Earl proceeded to kiss her on the thigh and up towards her pureness. He slipped his tongue around Tesha's outer lips, and he felt her quiver. As he continued to give Tesha her first lesson in cunnilingus, Earl knew that this would not be the last. She was so sweet on his tongue. Deep down he knew that he was probably wrong, but his mind was telling him that it was okay, especially since she didn't ask him to stop. Even from this angle, Tesha looked just like his first love… Chell.

For a second, Earl thought that he heard something and decided not to chance it and stopped. He kissed Tesha on her thighs and up her stomach. Once he reached her size "A" cups, he paused and looked up into her face and smiled. Earl continued up her neck and whispered in her ear "this is just between us."

"Why didn't you scream or run out of the bathroom?" Angie asked in a not too pleasant voice.

Tesha started to cry. She knew that Angie would be upset by her revelation, so she decided to leave out the part about her enjoying what Earl was doing to her.

"I was scared that you would be mad at me like you are now," Tesha said through tears.

Angie didn't really know what to do, but she knew that this had to be addressed. She got up and walked out, leaving Tesha alone without another word.

Angie told Earl that night that it would be best if he moved out until this situation was fixed. He honestly looked surprised when Angie told him what Tesha had said. He swore to God that he didn't do anything wrong to Tesha. Earl tried to blow off any accusations of there being more to the relationship by saying that the girl just liked being around him, but Angie was not moved this time. Earl decided to go along with Angie's request. He also knew that with a little time, Angie would let him come back home. He knew that she loved him too much to let something like this drive him away. Besides, he was the best thing that ever happened to her.

Later that week Angie took Tesha to the gynecologist for a complete physical exam and STD check. She didn't want to believe that Earl had touched the girl, but she also knew not to put it past him.

COLD BLOODED

*T*ime does not always heal all wounds. It has been over 20 years and I still feel like the black sheep of my family. My mama has always acted like she didn't want anything to do with me, but Chell on the other hand has always been treated like the special one. All my life I have been the good girl. I went to school, didn't get caught with boys or drugs, but that still was not enough to gain my mother's love. Chell did everything she could think of and my mother would have never known if I weren't there to enlighten her. I never thought of what I was doing as tattling as the kid's say; I was just being a good daughter and telling my mom what was going on behind her back. I knew that this would make her love me more because I was being honest with her and not sneaking around.

Now at 35 I am still going to be the informant;

it's just in my nature. I believe that everyone wants to know what is going on around them and if I know, why shouldn't I be the one to tell them. I am only being a good Christian by not letting my friends and family walk around blinded by Satan. That is after all what I'm supposed to do, right?

Angie recalled how Earl was always in a good mood when Tesha was around, and she wished that she could bring joy to his life like that. She felt that she had done the right thing by taking Tesha to the doctor and kicking Earl out of her house. She really feared that what Tesha told her was true, but she owed Earl the benefit of the doubt. It was all so confusing that she could not think straight. And telling anyone in my family was definitely not an option because then they would think that I can't control my own household.

At Dr. Holloway's office, Angie would not dare tell the doctor the truth behind their visit. Angie told the doctor that she thought Tesha was having sex and wanted to get her checked out and put on some birth control. Angie figured that if she told the doctor the truth, they would call Child Protective Services, and she could not have that happen. A week later, the doctor called Angie with the results of Tesha's exam.

"Hi, this is Dr. Holloway. I have some good news for you, Ms. Anderson."

"We'll see," commented Angie.

The doctor was a little put off by this, but she continued. "There was no evidence of sexual contact and since her hymen was still intact, there was no reason to believe that she was not still a virgin. But since you were concerned, do you still want to start her on birth control? If so, I can meet with you both in two weeks to discuss some options for Tesha."

"OK" was all Angie could muster before hanging up the phone.

Angie could not believe her ears. *When I get home I'm gonna kick her trick ass for lying to my face.*

Angie drove home as fast as she could with her mind set; she didn't want to hear anything Tesha had to say. It was already made up in her mind that her lil black ass was lying the whole time and trying to break up her and Earl.

Angie busted through Tesha's bedroom door and started in on her without missing a beat.

"Of all the things I've done for you, this is how you repay me...by lying."

"Auntie, what are you talking about?" Tesha was caught off guard and scared as hell!

"I talked to your doctor and she said nothing happened to you. Why did you make that up?"

"I didn't make it up. That did happen!" Tesha yelled.

"Then why didn't the doctor find anything, huh?"

"I don't know. Auntie please believe me," Tesha begged.

"I don't believe shit you say. You're just like your lying ass crack-whore of a mama. I ain't raising no whores up in here. I'ma put the spirit of God in yo ass yet. Get your black ass out of my house."

"Where am I gonna go?" The tears flowed like a river down Tesha's face. She could not understand why her aunt did not believe her. There was no reason for her to lie.

As Tesha went outside, Angie went into the kitchen. By the time Tesha made it down the steps, Angie was right behind her with an extension cord. She grabbed Tesha by the back of her neck and pulled her over to the nearest tree behind their house. Tesha was crying hysterically by now and was praying that Earl came back home. She thought that Angie was going to hang her up by her heels like she always threatened. Instead, she tied Tesha to the trunk of the tree with a clothes line that had fallen to the ground. She walked around to the side of the house and got the water hose and turned it on. Angie mumbled half prayers and half obscenities under her breath all the way there and all the way back.

She proceeded to wet Tesha up from head to toe with the water, still cuss-praying. It was like she was possessed. Tesha tried to wiggle free, but she could barely move because the ropes were too tight. After Tesha was soaked Angie picked up the extension cord and started to strike her over and over again. Tesha's cries turned into wails of pain. Angie kept on hitting her, showing no mercy. It seemed like hours had passed when Angie finally stopped striking her niece. She had given her ten lashings, one for each year she had been forced to care for her.

Tesha was about two lashings from passing out when the beating stopped. Angie untied her and walked away. She felt relieved as her body fell to the ground with a thud. She laid in the grass trying to stifle her moans of pain so that her aunt would not come back out there. Her body was consumed with pain, while her heart was filling with hate.

A neighbor had called Earl when they heard all the screaming and fussing to tell him to get over here quick, but he couldn't...he was in Georgia. Earl pulled up into the yard about two hours after Angie's rampage. As Earl turned in their drive-way, which was really just a slap of concrete that used to be the foundation of an old garage, his headlights reflected something in the back of the house, so he grabbed his gun and went to investigate. He was alarmed to find that it was Tesha. Tesha was still outside on the ground. She had fallen asleep under the tree because she was too scared to move.

"Tesha, what are you doing out here on the ground? Why are you wet?" he asked reaching for her.

Tesha slowly opened her eyes and blinked several times to get her focus. When she saw that it was Earl, a weak smile crossed her lips. When Earl touched her arm she let out a low yelp of pain; her body had welted all over by now. Earl instinctively let her go and jumped back and took a long look at her. He knew then what had happened.

"Tesha, can you move baby?"

"Help me up," she said barely above a whisper, her throat was dry as a desert.

Earl helped her up as gently as he could, trying not to cause her any more pain. Tears crept to the corners of his eyes, but he refused to let them fall. He helped Tesha into the house and put her in her room.

"I'll come back to take care of you…okay?" It was more of a question than a statement.

He turned off the light and backed out of the door.

"ANGIE, GET CHO ASS OUT HERE... NOW!"

"What are you yelling at me for?" Angie answered sitting in the dark room rocking in her favorite spot.

"What the hell is wrong with you? Why did you do that girl like that?" Earl said while turning on some lights.

"I was gonna call you. What are you doing here anyway?"

"Damn that, answer my question. Why did you do that to her?"

"She lied to me," Angie said nonchalantly.

"About what and don't you lie to *me*, Angie."

"About what I put you out for, that's what. If she wasn't up in your ass all the damn time I would'na had to take her to the doctor. The doctor said that nothing happened to Tesha, so I beat her ass for lying."

"I told you that I didn't do nothing wrong. Your stupid ass should have left it at that, but no you had to try and find some shit. Like I said befo', Tesha just likes to hang around me because she ain't got nobody else. She tryna find herself. You got her so scared of you that she don't know which way is up. You're always so mean to the girl, so she tries to stay out of your way, but you still go looking for shit. Now you better stop looking 'cause you might not like what you find."

"And what's that suppose to mean?" Angie asked as she looked up at Earl.

"Just what I said…stop looking for shit."

Angie just sat there. She knew deep down that what she had done was wrong. She didn't feel bad for beating Tesha, actually it felt good. It was like all the pent up frustrations were released with every blow. She hated that Earl was mad at her though. She had to smooth things over with him. In her mind, Tesha was standing in her way of happiness and that was a bigger problem than him being mad at her. Something had to be done about her.

For the next few weeks, Earl stopped by after work to nurse Tesha back to health. He and Angie were just passing by each other in the house like strangers. She was too afraid to say anything to him, and he was too disgusted to say anything to her. Tesha took this time to think about what she was going to do to get her aunt back for what she had done to her. She knew that someone would have to teach Angie's mean, hateful ass a lesson on how to treat people. Tesha asked Earl to never mention this to anyone because she didn't want them to take her away to a foster home. He promised because he didn't want that to happen either; plus he knew that he was the only one who could protect her.

After being gone for over a month, Earl moved back in and things were pretty much back to normal around there. Angie and Earl were on speaking terms again. She even started speaking to Tesha again; well, it was more like ordering her around again. The night Earl moved back in, he and Angie took a drive to discuss the conditions that he would stay with her. After driving to the old camp ground in the next town, they pulled in and parked.

"Earl, why did we come here?"

"So that we could talk without any interruptions," he answered calmly.

Angie knew better. It was more so that they wouldn't have any witnesses. The years that they have been together has taught Angie that the only reason Earl allows her to talk shit and humiliate him in public was because he always knew how to get her back...in private. She knew that the whole Tesha thing was not over. It was only a matter of time before he wanted to "talk" to her in private.

"What do you want to talk about honey? I thought that we already decided that we were ok 'cause you moved back in?"

"Yeah we did, but I'm not staying until we get some things straight."

"Okay," Angie said sounding very nervous while anticipating Earl's next move.

"I don't want you to touch Tesha ever again," he said calmly.

"I take care of her and I will discipline her ass whenever I damn well see fit!" Angie said folding her arms across her chest.

"Like I said Angie, I don't want you to touch her again. It's not up for discussion."

"Like I said Earl, I—"

Her wind was cut off.

Earl's grip around Angie's thick neck was not to be taken as a joke. He didn't say anything for about 10 seconds; he just stared at Angie with rage in his eyes. He leaned in close to Angie as if someone else might hear him.

"Don't you ever put your got-damned hands on her again, do you hear me bitch?" he shook her with every other word and when she didn't reply, he squeezed her tighter.

"I said do you hear me bitch?" Earl yelled into Angie's ear.

Angie could not breathe, and her tears stung her eyes before they fell down her checks. She knew that if she didn't comply that he may just kill her and leave her in the woods. So she nodded in agreement the best way that she could because his grip on her neck never let up.

"If you ever touch her again bitch, I'll kill you!"

With that, Earl released his death grip on Angie's neck. He started the car and headed home. A silent Angie sat next to him in a daze wondering how her life ended up like this.

GET YOUR HOUSE
IN ORDER

*A*s the months passed Earl and Tesha had resumed their leisure activities of fishing and hunting trips. While out one day, Earl asked her about what happened with Angie.

"Tesha, why did you tell Angie what happened in the bathroom?" quizzed Earl.

"I don't know. She just asked me and I told her."

"Look, what happens between us should stay between us. Angie will always overreact; you see what happened. I'm not saying that you should lie to her, but damn, learn to keep your mouth shut."

"Ok, Uncle Earl."

"And stop calling me that," he snapped. He saw that this took the shine out of her eyes and knew if he wanted her back on his team, he'd have to play nice.

"Look, T-Baby, don't look so sad. It's just that when you call me that, it makes how I feel about you seem so wrong. I'm not your uncle, so don't call me that when we are alone. I know what your auntie did to you was messed up, but you don't have to worry about that ever happening again," said Earl.

"How you know that? She knew that you wouldn't be back, so that's why she did it then. Every time you leave me, she starts acting all crazy. She calls me names in front of her friends and always is trying to put me down," Tesha said gazing out at the lake.

"Well, you don't have to worry about Angie for too much longer because she knows that her ass is mine if she ever so much as thinks about touching you again. Just stick with me and do what I say… you won't have to worry about nothin' baby," he said with a smirk as he rubbed her leg.

That news made Tesha feel all warm and fuzzy inside. If she didn't know before, she knew it now-- he loved her. He may be with Angie physically, but his heart is with her. He always knew what to say to make her feel better. They continued to talk about life and how good it would be without Angie around to bother them. On the way back home, they rode around the back roads drinking on some *Paul* and enjoying life in their own world. The more Earl talked to Tesha, the more control he had over her. She became his puppet. In Tesha's eyes, Earl alone was her world and nothing else mattered.

Earl promised Tesha the world if she cooperated with him. He told her all about the money that he could give her and how good her life would be with him in the end. Eventually, he had even convinced her that her family was against her. They didn't want to see her happy and that's why they always had something to say about them. Tesha could do whatever she wanted when they were together. Earl never played the role of the father; it was like they were just buddies hanging out. Earl taught her life lessons on how a man is supposed to treat a lady and what a lady is to do for her man. Other lessons included how to behave around Angie and the family so that they would mind their business.

During the next few months, physical contact between Earl and Tesha was kept at a minimum. Earl didn't want to rush Tesha into anything until after she was a little older. He knew that right now they could not prove anything, and he knew that if someone said anything that she would deny it. This thing with Tesha was working out real good. Earl gave Tesha a separate allowance of $100 a month. She listened to him and did whatever he asked of her without any questions. Tesha was on cloud 9. When she did something good for him, he rewarded her with gifts and extra money; he even bought her a cell phone. The phone was a gift after she let him finger her. He told to her to keep the phone a secret because if Angie knew about it, she would surely take it.

When they were apart, this was their primary method of communication. What Tesha didn't realize was that the reason behind the phone was to keep track of her and to find out what Angie was doing. Earl never planned to leave Angie. Why should he? Lately she has been pretty quiet. She got her a new job at the casino, and she started to make house calls for her hair appointments instead of letting them come to the house because of a little incident with one of her good friends and Earl. All her time out of the house left Earl home alone with Tesha for most of the day. They didn't mind; the house was much quieter with her gone anyway.

Angie was on a mission to get herself together. She was the first one up and the last one to bed.

With the problems at home, she decided that it was best that she spent as little time there as she could. She and Earl were talking again, but anyone could see the tension in the air. Tesha was different also. Her attitude had taken on a life of its own; she did not have a fear of Angie anymore. To anyone on the outside it looked more like Tesha was the lady of the house and Angie was the visitor. While Angie was away, Tesha ran the house and was never too far from Earl. And when they were home, Tesha was always right by his side. All the seats in the living room could be free, but if he was sitting on the love seat, she would slide right in next to him. Angie never parted her lips, just sat back watching and rocking.

Angie knew how her situation must look, but she refused to give in. She had something to prove to those with doubt that she and Earl's relationship was solid. Earl must still love her because if he didn't, why is he still here? As long as he was in their house, she still had a chance to get him back. The wheels were turning in her head as she tried to think of a way to get Earl to start paying more attention to her. But that would have to wait because she had a customer coming by for a roller set. Lately, she went to her client's house but this lady was known to have a nasty house with roaches. So this time she made an exception because she didn't want any hitchhikers.

"Hey, Mrs. Rose," Angie said opening the door wide so she could see what Earl was doing outside also.

"Whew, girl I almost didn't make it."

"Well, I'm glad you did, come on in and have a seat," Angie instructed with a wave of her hand.

"So what's new Angie?" Rose asked making herself comfortable at the kitchen table.

"Not much, you know the same old thang," said Angie while setting out her hair supplies.

"Are we alone?" asked Mrs. Rose as she looked around the room.

"Yeah, Earl and Tesha are outside under the tree."

"Well, that is what I wanted to talk to you about," said Mrs. Rose.

Damn here she go. If I woulda known she wanted to get in my business, I would have cancelled this appointment.

"What's on your mind, Mrs. Rose?"

"You know that there has been a lot of talk around here about them two."

Angie just listened while she scratched Rose's scalp. She did this for her older customers because they liked to get the dandruff up before their washing.

"I don't like to be talking behind nobody's back, so I figured that I'd come talk to you myself to see if I could help in anyway," stated Mrs. Rose.

Angie was a bit surprised by her last statement; she just knew that she was going to go throwing around accusations.

"Mrs. Rose, I can assure you that there is nothing going on with them two. You know that Tesha doesn't know her father. So to her Earl is like a dad that's all."

"But why are they always together? I have girls too and they aint never run up behind they daddy like that."

"They work together too."

"Now you know what I'm talking about, child, so don't play with me. I see them all the time in town, Tesha driving and Earl lying back trying not to be seen. They are doing more than working together, and I think you know that."

Now Mrs. Rose was standing up looking Angie square in her face.

"Mrs. Rose, I have asked them and they both say that nothing is going on. What else am I supposed to do?" she asked turning the water on in the sink.

"All I'm saying is for you to keep your eyes open. Okay. Don't put anything past a man baby.

We all have our burdens. Don't make more for yourself than you already have because you will regret not taking action sooner. Now I'm telling you what I know, not what I heard. That's all I have to say about that."

Mrs. Rose bent her head in the sink for her washing and was glad that she said her peace. Angie thought about what was said, and she knew that it was right. The only problem was that if she takes any action, it will be like saying that everyone is right about them. She just could not take that right now. *Everything done in the dark will come to light, with or without my help,* thought Angie.

Bridge Over Troubled Waters

The seasons came and went and all was peaceful in the Wright household. Christmas was right around the corner, and Angie was in full shopping mode. Every day, she went to work, shopping, and the casino. She developed the gambling habit after Earl's discussion with her in the car. Shopping and gambling had become forms of therapy that were used to with how she felt about Earl and Tesha. They continued to be closer than they should, but there was nothing Angie could do. If she made any type of fuss, he would leave her and then their secret would be out to everyone.

Angie sat in her designated seat in front of their large picture frame window in the living room. This was her favorite seat in the house because she could see all of the comings and goings of the neighborhood. Their house sat across the street from the corner store. There was always something going on over at that store. The Mitchell Brothers Quick Stop was the only store that sold alcohol within walking distance, so it was frequented by all the local drunks, booze hags, and hustlers. This seat was also a prime location to look at the tree that Earl and Tesha always sat under when they were drinking and smoking.

I am not even gonna worry about Tesha's and Earl's trifling asses. They think they're hurting somebody, but they ain't hurting nobody but themselves. I can't believe that they would do this to me after all that I have done for them. I took Earl in off the streets when he got out of jail and provided for him because he couldn't get a job right away. And Tesha, only God knows where she would be if she was still with that crack-head of a mama. She ain't nothing but a trick baby anyway, and I don't see what Earl sees in her anyway. I still don't regret what I did to her because she deserved it. Hell, she probably asked him to come into the bathroom with her, like mother like daughter. Earl used to tell me that Chell would throw herself at him all the time. He is a man; what was he supposed to do? If a woman is throwing the ass around, what man is going to say "no thanks, I'm good"? Not many. I don't even blame him; I blame Tesha for being such a whore just like her mammy.

To be honest, I don't even see the big deal because he didn't *really* have sex with her anyway. Tesha wouldn't be all up under Earl if he had actually hurt her. It's not like he stuck it in her; plus she is a big girl now, and she can handle it.

Angie sat and reflected on her life…

It was the summer of 1982, and me and Chell were spending our vacation with our great grandparents on their farm here in Maplesville. We used to always like coming down here because we could basically run wild. Grandpa was usually in the field while Grandma was in the house, so we kids had the run of the land with no parental supervision. It was the real country. There were pigs, cows, chickens, turkeys, and horses on the farm. The fowls roamed free, so you had to be careful as to not step in some shit. Every once in a while, the pigs and hogs would get out and chase us around the house; that was really fun. My mama didn't have anything to worry about because she knew that we were in good hands with Grandma.

Grandma had seven children with Grandpa, and as quiet as it was kept, only four of them were his. Anyway, all of them were grown and some of them even had children of their own. Every summer, all the grandkids would come down and stay until the family reunion at the end of the summer. Only three of Grandma's children lived close by. My aunt stayed next door in an old single-wide trailer when she was home-- she had a habit of just taking off and leaving her two daughters behind for months at a time. My uncle stayed about 10 minutes away with his wife and two children who practically lived on the farm. My other uncle lived in the back room with his wife and their three kids. There was always someone there and always some kids to play with; that's why we loved it down here so much.

One cool summer morning, I got up early so that I could go pick some berries before it got too hot. I woke Chell up so that she could come with me, but she had snuck out the night before and was still drunk from hanging out with Jessie and his friends at the lake. I got on up, took my wash-up, and got dressed. Grandma and Grandpa were already up and beginning their day. I kissed Grandma on the cheek and told her that I was going to pick me some muscadines. I didn't want to walk the dirt road to the berry patch, so I took a short cut through the woods. I could get to the berry bushes in about 10 minutes instead of the 20 it would take if I went around the long way.

I made it to the patch just as the weather started to warm up. In the south, the sun is shining good by 10am, so me leaving out a little after 8 would give me enough time to pick my berries and get home before I had a heat stroke. I knew these woods like the back of my hand. Me and my cousins used to always play around here looking for snakes and climbing trees. Well, they used to climb trees; I wasn't getting my big butt up in no tree. I have always been chubby, even as a child. This was not always a burden; it afforded me some luxuries too. I wasn't liked by my other female cousins because they could only go out if they took me with them. My grandma used to always say that I was her favorite because I was a good girl unlike my other cousins who were always chasing after boys. My grandma was the only person who really appreciated me, and I was the only one there during her last days.

Just as I was picking my last berry, I heard someone call my name. I turned around, but there was nobody there. I heard it again behind me and I spun around just in time to see Arnez Johnson, or Nez for short. Nez was my best girlfriend. Her folks lived up the road, and her family had more kids than mine, it was a whole gang of them. She was a few years older than me, but we didn't care. I never really had many friends because most kids used to tease me about my skin color or my weight. Arnez was different. Most of the time we would just talk mess about other people and play by our favorite place, ol' Minnie's Creek. It was named that after a little girl drowned in it before I was born.

"Hey, Annie, what's up?" asked Nez. She was the only person who could call me Annie.

"Not much, Nez, just picking me some berries. What chu doing out here?"

"Nothin' just out here with my cousins playin'. You out here byuaself?" she asked in a heavy southern drawl.

"Yeah, but I'ma 'bout to head back; it's starting to get hot out here," I said shielding my eyes from the sun.

There was a sparkle in Arnez's eyes when I told her I was here by myself. She must have some juicy gossip to share.

"Annie, you don't have-ta-go-now do ya? Why don't you come play with us for a while?"

It was not really a question because Nez was already pulling me towards the nearby laughter.

I didn't want to go play with no other children

because they were always teasing me. Me and Nez hadn't played together much this summer, so I went anyway. We went down by the creek, and there were about 5 other kids already there swimming. It was a mix of girls and boys, so I was a little more relaxed; plus some of them were Arnez's kin folks. They really didn't pay me any mind, so I felt safe. Nez knew that I couldn't swim, so we just sat down on the bank and put our feet in the water.

"Girl, did you hear what happened to my cousin Paulette?"

"Naw, what?" I asked offering her some of my berries.

"Chris went upside that head, that's what."

"What! I didn't know nuttin 'bout that."

"Yeah girl, somebody told him that she was messin' round with Johnnie Lee."

I don't know what my cousin Chris ever saw in her because she was thin as a twig and black as coal. Her hair was nappy as a sheep's coat. Her teeth were bucked from sucking her thumb, something she still did when she thought no one was watching. I told Chris that girl was no good because I saw her with Johnny Lee one night down at the lake. I told him how she was all hugged up with that Lee boy, but he didn't want to believe me. I hope Chris didn't tell Paulette that I was the one who told on her. Nez thought to herself.

"Is she alright? Do they know who told him that mess?"

"Naw! She's ok, but he blacked her eye real good. I was sure that you heard about it."

"Naw, If I did I'd sho nuff tell you. That's real messed up tho"

"Sho' is," Nez said through sucks on a handful of my berries.

The other kids had run off back into the woods by now and it was just me and Nez, just how I wanted it.

"Hey, Annie, I'ma be right back, my mama is calling me," Nez yelled to me as she ran off.

"Ok."

I washed some more of my berries in the creek and sat with my back up against a nearby log. I'm gonna eat these then grab some more on my way back home. Just as I was about to put the last berry in my mouth, I heard someone whistling. I didn't know who it was, so I stood up and started to head home.

"You whoooo," a male voice said in a sing-song tone.

I kept walking.

"I said, you whoooo gal. I know you hear me."

I turned around and saw one of Nez's boy

cousins standing with two other boys I didn't know. My heart was beating out of my chest, so I waved hello and started walking as fast as I could towards my granny's house. I heard twigs crunching under running feet, so I dropped the rest of my uneaten berries and started running. I don't know if I fell over something or if someone grabbed my leg. All I remember is falling on my face with a hard thud. The boy that called me was on my back pushing my face in the dirt.

"So you like telling on people, huh?"

I started to scream but he mushed my face into the dirt sideways.

"We gonna teach your ass a lesson about tattling on folks. Nez told us that you were the one who told we took Ol Man Tucker's truck for a joyride and it ended up in the river."

Nez set me up for a beating. Ooh wait 'till I see her ass again.

"STOP IT...YOU'RE HURTING ME!" I screamed

"You ain't hurt yet; get your fat ass up."

I stood up and looked around to get my bearings. I tried to take a mental picture of the boys so that I could tell my uncles who they were so that they could kick they ass. I thought about running again, but I was already out of breath and they had me surrounded. Every time I tried to get out of the circle they made around me, one would push me back in the middle. They called me every name but a child of God. I didn't know what else to do but cry for help, but we were in the woods. Who would hear me?

"I swear I won't tell nothing else ever again, I promise," I cried.

"We know you won't 'cause if you do, we gonna drown your big ass in that der creek. I know you don't know how to swim, so it'll be easy," one of the other boys said laughing.

I tried to make a run for it again but got thrown to the ground with a kick to my butt. I tried to get up, but they were on me. I fought them off the best I could but I was out of breath. My arms were snatched up over my head and my feet were held down by the two boys I didn't know.

"You like running your mouth, huh? HUH!" he yelled.

I shook my head no because I was afraid to speak.

"Open your mouth."

When I didn't do as he said, he started slapping my face. Wack! Wack! Wack! I tasted blood in my mouth!

"Open your mouth," he commanded.

I didn't want him to hit me again so I did as he

said and opened my mouth. When I did, he shoved his ding-dong in my mouth and told me to suck it. I started gagging. I thought he was trying to choke me with it. I could not breathe. I tried to wiggle my head so that I could spit it out, but he grabbed my face and held it in place. I started choking, so he let me go. When he moved his ding-a-ling, I started screaming bloody murder.

"I see you still didn't learn your lesson," he laughed in my face as he was standing up over me.

I closed my eyes anticipating the next blow, but it didn't come just yet. I heard something wet splash on the ground next to my face and one of the guys started laughing real loud. I opened my eyes and the one with the nasty wee-wee was peeing around my head. When I opened my eyes he took aim at my face, and I started gasping for air. Piss landed in my mouth and my eyes….I tried to scream, but the urine started going down my throat causing me to cough.

When he moved away from me, I thought the worst was over, but I was mistaken. He switched places with the one holding my feet. This boy was older than them. He had hair on his face and at first I didn't recognize him. But when he got closer, I saw something familiar in his eyes. A rush of relief swept over my body, but it was taken away as soon as I saw him unzipping his pants. I cannot believe this is about to happen to me. I started to scream, but the boy holding my hands covered my mouth. I let the tears flow, and I yelled for God to help. My body went numb. One after the other, they raped me. That was the day my spirit was broken. After those animals finished stealing my innocence, they left me there in the grass beaten and bloody without a second thought.

The ringing of the phone brought Angie back to reality. She answered the phone while wiping her tears away with the back of her hand. It was her girlfriend Nay, who no doubt wanted to go to the casino. Angie ended the call with an "ok". She took $200 from Earl's stash that he thought she didn't know about, grabbed her purse, and hit the streets.

Stranger in My House

"Tesha, come here!" Angie yelled from her bedroom snapping Tesha out of her thoughts.

"Yes, ma'am," she said as she sprang to her feet.

"What is this doing in here?" Angie asked holding up Tesha's bracelet.

"I was looking for that, Auntie; I must have lost it when I was cleaning in here," Tesha said nervously as she took the bracelet from Angie's grasp. She knew good and well that she lost it… just not cleaning. Tesha had been looking for her bracelet for over a week, and she knew that when Angie found it, she must have lost it the last time her and Earl had one of their lessons.

Tesha thinks her ass is nickel slick. I know that something is going on no matter what they say. But what am I supposed to do? I don't have any proof, but that nigga gonna slip up, and I'll be right there waiting. Angie thought to herself while shaking her head.

"Earl, I think it is time for Tesha to go stay with her mother." Angie said the words that she had been rehearsing for the past few weeks. She knew that Earl would not like it, but what was he going to do? They were leaving first light whether he liked it or not.

"Why? We have been seeing after her for all these years, what you wanna send her home for?" Earl asked not looking up from the TV.

Earl knew what Angie was trying to do, but he also knew that he had to play it cool because if he objected too much, it would look suspicious.

"Well, her mom is doing better now, and she should have a relationship with her." Angie knew taking the angle of looking out for Tesha's best interest would do the trick.

"Did you ask Tesha if she wanted to go? I mean ain't no reason to *force* the girl." Earl laughed to himself and thought two can play that game, so he pulled the best interest card also.

"No, I didn't ask her, but she is the child and we are the adults. Plus, I figured that we could take advantage of the time and finally get married. You remember, you promised me that when the time was right, we would do it and what better time than over the summer. It don't have to be anything big. We can fly to Vegas and spend the weekend in the casino.

Earl took in what Angie was saying and was trying to figure a way out of it. He didn't want to marry Angie. But lately that was all that she had been talking about. He knew that if he wanted the comforts that he had grown accustomed to, he would have to do something. He just wasn't sure if jumping the broom was the right answer. Telling her no was going to be a fight, so he had to choose his words wisely.

"Angie, what's the rush with getting married?" Earl asked stalling for time.

"What the hell do you mean rush? We have been shacking up for over 15 years. Don't you think that it is time?"

"We already do everything that married couples do, so what do you need a piece of paper for? Everybody knows that we are together and neither one of us is going anywhere. I don't see what the big deal is anyway."

"The big deal is that we need to live right under God."

"Oh, don't go throwing God into this. We have been living and lovin' in sin for as you said over 15 years. You just want to put a low-jack on a nigga and I ain't having it."

"Oh, you ain't having it, or you just don't want to stop fucking around?" Angie knew that this would get him going. Earl hated being accused of cheating, even if it were true.

"Here you go with this shit again. Angie, I ain't fucking around, I just ain't ready to get married yet. Baby, you know I love you, right?" he asked looking Angie deep in her eyes. He knew this always worked because she thought she could always tell when he was lying by looking in his eyes. He had perfected his sincere leer over the years, and it never failed him.

"Yeah, Earl, I know you love me, but I want the world to know it too. Is that so wrong?" Angie said through tears. "Earl, if you don't want to marry me just say so and I will move on. I'm tired of people talking behind my back saying that you don't really want to be with me. You need to prove them wrong or else I'm gone. By the way, I don't want Tesha in my damn room when I'm not here." With that said, Angie walked out the door, slamming it behind her.

Even with all the mess going on I love Earl and have always wanted a man like him. He loves me for who I am no matter what. Hell, I was the chosen one after all. My sister always had the good men, but this time, the good man picked me over her. And as long as I live, we will be together and nothing is going to stop our love. I know that I have to do something with Tesha before she ruins my life. Angie thought to herself as she headed to the casino.

Earl knew that he would have to do something because his disability settlement was just around the corner and he was going to need someone to take care of him until it came through. After having to shut down his business so that they could see that he didn't have any income, he knew that Angie was all he had. Tesha was cool, but she couldn't take care of him like a mama should and Angie would. Hell, Tesha couldn't see to his every need. Angie was conditioned already and she knew just what he liked. Last year when Earl had to have back surgery, Angie took care of him. She handled all the household chores and made sure that he didn't lift a finger all while working a full time job.

❧

"Tesha, how did she know that you were in our room?" Earl asked while on a drive to the truck stop for some beer…it was cheaper in town than next door.

"She found my bracelet."

"Damn girl, you got to be more careful. You gone get both our asses put out. Then what?"

"I'm sorry," she said rubbing his leg as he drove.

"From now on, I'll come to your room," Earl said as he made a left turn on Main Street.

"What if she catches us?" she asked sitting up straight.

"Angie ain't thinking about us; long as she get paid, she is all good."

Relaxing back in her seat, Tesha said quietly, "Money ain't everything."

"Bullshit! When you ain't got it, it is. Money makes the world go round. Why do you think she still around here?"

"I thought it was because she loves you," Tesha added as she picked her finger nail polish.

"Looka here, girl, and let me explain something to you." He patted the steering wheel like a drum.

"Angie don't love nobody but herself. We have been together for years, and it is a partnership not a relationship. We watch each other's back, you know, like family. In this partnership needs have to be met. We can't afford to bring any ol' body up in here, so we satisfy each other's needs. You understand?"

Tesha looked confused. "Then why am I here?" she asked.

"Because you need somebody to take care of you. I am going to always take care of you. I know that you like being here with me, and I like having you here. Over the years, I have seen you grow from a child to a young woman, and I can't help but to feel something different for you." Earl rubbed her knee for extra emphasis. "I love you, Tesha."

Tesha's heart melted. She had never had anyone tell her that they loved her, not even her mother. She liked the feelings that it gave her. Earl made her feel safe, and he never treated her like a child like everyone else did. Maybe if she played her cards right Earl would make her his partner and get rid of Angie. "I love you, too, Earl."

Let's Chill

"Earl, we need to talk."

"Bout what?"

"Can you come sit with me for a sec?"

"Nah, I can hear you from here…what chu wont?"

"I'm pregnant."

"What?"

"I went to the doctor yesterday and I'm 3 months pregnant, that's what."

"Well, that is something to talk about. Considering you told me you can't have no kids," said Earl.

"I guess God has other plans, cause I am," said Angie.

Earl quickly took a seat on the sofa next to his future baby mama. He could not believe his ears. He always wanted to be a father, but after all this time, he had given up on the idea. Those two around the corner didn't count because he didn't believe that they were his anyway, so this would be his first child. In a way, Earl was excited. A smile crept across his face before he spoke again.

"I guess that means that we may as well get married, huh?"

"Do you really mean it baby?" asked an excited Angie.

"Yes, I do."

"Earl slid off the sofa and got down on one knee and grabbed his bride to be by the hand. Baby, I know that I have been a hard man to love, and I'm sorry. I want to do this family thing the right way. I know that I can be a good daddy and a good husband if you let me. Baby, will you let me?"

The tears fell from Earl's eyes putting the icing on his proposal. Before she spoke, Angie took a deep breath and smiled. This was all that she had dreamed of and more.

"Yes, Earl, I will marry you."

Earl got up off the floor and kissed and hugged Angie with new found passion. Angie could not wait to tell everyone she knew. Her first call was going to be to her mom and then she would rub her news in Chell's face and send Tesha packing for good. Angie would start planning her Vegas wedding first thing in the morning. She knew she could convince Earl of a quick wedding by using the pregnancy as a reason to rush things along.

UnBreak My Heart

I can't believe that this day has finally come. I will be a married woman in 24 hours! I prayed and prayed that God would hear my cry and send me a husband. Now I have what I have always wanted. Earl may not be the man of my dreams, but he is my man and I love him. I know that in the past we have had our ups and downs, but now all that has changed. When he asked me to marry him, I was so excited. After 6 weeks, here we are in Las Vegas ready to do the damn thang!

I have done everything I could to make this a day to remember for the both of us. I have flown in my mother and my Madea to be our witnesses. I paid for his tux rental and shoes. I already had my dress because I knew that after 15 years, this day would eventually come.

I have reserved our rooms and I plan on spending the weekend here and burning up the casinos.

Some people drink or smoke, but I play the slots. I'm gonna go check on Mama and Madea and make sure that they are settling in alright. Maybe we can get some action in on the machines. Those two are probably already at the slots because they love them more than I do.

"What chu hens up to?"Angie asked opening the door to her mother Maggie's room.

"Nothing but waiting for you. What took you so long?" Mama asked me while putting the finishing touches on her make-up.

My mother Maggie, Mags for short, still looked good at 50. By her still living in Bolingbrook, we don't get to see much of each other. I try to call her every day to find out what's new. I know that she has not been feeling well lately, so hopefully this trip will brighten her spirits. She tries to down play her illness, but when I look into her eyes, I see that it hurts her more than she wants to let on.

Mags is a severe diabetic, but she acts like nothing is wrong. Mags still smokes a pack of *Kool's* a day and drinks RC soda by the case load. She doesn't eat well because she says that the food makes her sick, and to top it off, her vision is getting bad. I keep trying to get her to move in with me and Earl, but she won't have it. And her excuse is always the same, "I got Chell to see about me" or "something wrong with that boy". But that something ain't ever stopped her from taking his money when she does visit. Where does she think I get the money for us to gamble? Mama always talking about Chell this and Chell that. I am so sick of her always devoting her attention to Chell's crack-head ass when I'm the one who takes care of her.

"Well, I'm here now so let's go." Angie said grabbing Mags and Madea by the arm.

"Why ain't nonna Earl's folks here?" Madea asked as we boarded the elevator.

"They couldn't get off work with this being last minute and all," Angie said looking away. That was not all a lie. They could not get off work, but what I left out was that Earl did not tell them that we were getting married. He said it was because they don't like me. And you know what? I didn't like their messy asses either.

"But its yawl's wedding!"

"I know. But you know how black people get… they don't ever want to see somebody else happy."

"Yeah I know but his mom should be here at least, I –"

"We're here, so stop the chatter and let's get some money" I said quickly changing the subject.

Madea can be noisy as hell. I'm glad that his family didn't come cause they are too messy. I know that they don't like me and I don't give a damn. After to-morrow I'm going to be here for good so they had better get used to it or get over it.

❧

"Earl, are you ready yet? We only have two hours to be at the chapel!" I yelled from the shower. I am so excited that I don't know what to do first. I bet Earl is dragging around as usual.

As I stepped out of the shower, I saw that Earl was getting dressed in his all white tux. He looked very handsome. I see why all the women around the way want him. After today, he is all mine and I will beat any bitch down who want to test me.

"Ann, I'm going down to the gift shop for some smokes, and I will meet you there," Earl said over his shoulder before he left the room.

What the hell he going to the store for? That shit can wait. I wonder why I bother with him sometimes. All I know is that he better not be late. While I'm talking, I better not be late. I have to get my make-up on which won't take much. My hair was already done, and before we left, I got a manicure and pedicure. Damn I look good!

With one last look in the mirror, Angie was out the door to become Mrs. Earl Wright.

The chapel was next door to the hotel that we were staying at, it was a bit cheesy but it would have to do. My mom looked nice in her peach dress and matching bag. Madea was just as cute with her baby blue two piece dress and matching hat. She thought she was cute too, sashaying through the chapel like this was her day instead of mine. I must admit my granny is still a hot mess. Everyone was present and accounted for except for Earl.

"Ann, where your man at?"

I knew nothing would get by Madea. "He's coming, Madea. He's probably in the bathroom primping or something." I don't know who I was trying to convince more, her or myself.

An hour later, still no Earl. This better not be happening. I am going to kill his black ass! Who the hell do he think he is? I called the room, nothing...I paged him, nothing...I called his cell phone, nothing. Where could he be? When I see his cat mouth ass, it is going to be on! I had to get away from Mags and Madea because I knew that they would question me to no end. So I stormed out of the chapel in an Oscar winning fashion before they could ask me anything. I didn't need this, not now. Today was supposed to be perfect, but it has turned into a bad dream.

I must have stormed into every casino on the

strip in my wedding dress looking for Earl. When I returned to the hotel several hours later, my whole body ached. My feet hurt from pounding the pavement, my back hurt from all this tension, my head hurt from crying, and my heart hurt from Earl. I felt so stupid. I cannot believe that he left me at the altar. I know one thing; his ass is going to pay me back all the money I've lost or I'm going to jail.

I slid my key card into the door and to my surprise there was Earl sitting on the bed, on the phone as if nothing had happened. This nigga must have a death wish. I'm going to be cool because if I lose it we're gonna end up on *CSI*.

"You must have went back home for those cigarettes?" Angie asked as she entered the room.

He just looked at her and went back to his conversation.

"Earl, you have some explaining to do, so get off the phone," Angie said as calmly as she could.

After hanging up the phone, he just looked at her. Angie wanted to knock his head off for embarrassing her in front of her family.

"Well?" Angie yelled.

"Well what?" Earl asked taking a puff from his cigarette.

"Where have you been, Earl?"

"Down stairs."

"Doing what?"

"Playing the slots."

"Is that where you were supposed to be today?"

"That's where I wanted to be." He said this all without ever looking up from the television.

"Look, I have been as calm as I can, but I see that you want to play games. Is that it? So you telling me that I have spent thousands of dollars on this trip for us to get married and all you can say is that you wanted to play slots instead? Have you lost your fucking mind! If your black ass didn't want to get married, why didn't you just say so?"

By now my cool is out the window and his ass is about to go with it. I cannot believe him!

"Angie, I tried to tell you that I wasn't ready to get married, but you kept on pushing me...I got scared baby. I'm sorry."

"Fuck sorry. Sorry didn't waste my money and my time. Sorry didn't make me look like a damn fool today, and sorry won't get you out of this shit. How could you do this to me, Earl? Don't you love me?" she said through teary eyes.

"Yes, baby, I just don't want to be rushed. Can't you understand that?"

"I understand but damn Earl it has been 15 years, how much time do you need?" trying to sound more understanding than sarcastic.

"I don't know, Angie. I just want it to be right, and this is not right. We have only been talking about this for two months. I couldn't even put no money on this with you. You were so excited, and I just couldn't stop you."

My heart was melting, but I refused to give in to his sly words.

"Earl, we decided that I would pay for the wedding and you would pay for the honeymoon. When did you change the plan?" Angie said as she sat down on the bed next to him.

"Baby, I had all intension of marring you today, but after I left this morning, I had some time to think things over. I know you deserve more than I have to give right now. I want to make you and the baby happy. I just cannot do it right now," said Earl.

He sounds so sincere. My mama always said that you have to work through the bad times so that you can experience the good. I don't mind being patient and helping my man out because it will be for the greater good. I'm glad that Earl wanted us to keep this a secret and make it a surprise to all our other family and friends because I don't know how I would hold my head up back home. Besides, he's right, we didn't plan this all out. I wanted to be married so bad that I didn't even think of his feelings. I am not going to lose

*my man over this. But what I am going to do is find
out who was so important that he had to call before
he talked to me. I know something is up because he
was just as excited as I was when we left home, but
now everything has changed. I will get to the bottom
of this.*

That night Angie was awakened with a sharp
pain in her abdomen. As she got up from the bed,
she saw that she was covered in blood. She screamed
for Earl to wake up and help her. With the amount
of blood that she lost, they both knew what was
happening. A midnight ER visit confirmed their
suspicions…the baby was gone.

YOU TALK TOO MUCH

a few months had passed since the fiasco in Vegas. Due to the miscarriage, Angie started doing hair at home again so that she could take it easy. Angie was quickly feeling better and keeping up mess as usual.

Some bad habits are hard to break and Angie had a bad habit of showing out in front of company. No matter who was at their house, she would have to talk about somebody's business. Everyone would laugh and kept her going. Today, Sister McCloud from church was the topic of discussion. Her husband had just been caught with the neighborhood sissy, Tweet. They called him Tweet because he knew all the down low men in town and said that he would sing like a bird if ever pushed.

"Girl, did you hear about Sister McCloud's husband?" she asked while hot curling Lisa's hair.

"Girl, no, what happened?"

"His stupid ass got caught with Tweet coming out of the Best Western."

"Whaaat…when this happen?" Lisa asked while holding her ear as not to get it burned by Angie's curling iron.

"Saturday night."

"Who told you that, Angie? You know how folks like to lie."

"This came from Sister McCloud herself. See I was tightening her wig at church, and she just broke down. When I asked her what was wrong, she just laid all his shit out there. Said the police came to her house with Lester in tow, talking about him and Tweet was outside the motel fighting."

"What was they fighting 'bout?"

"She said Tweet was going to tell on his dirty ass because he tried to skip out without paying him for his "services.""

"Girl, what she gonna do now?"

"I don't even know, but knowing her sanctified tail, she gonna keep him and just pray about it."

"Damn that! If it was me he would be out the door on his sissy ass."

"Who you telling? I'd have to go upside that head first then kick him out. He wants to be a bitch; I'll treat him like one." They both burst out laughing at this.

As Lisa said her goodbye's, Angie thought to herself that Lisa doesn't have any room to talk because her man cheats so much that you can't tell his wife from his mistress or his mistress from his jump-off. Folks always talking about what they would do if it were them. You could never know how you would react to a situation until it actually happens to you.

In front of her friends, Angie treated Tesha like shit. She was always calling her a nappy head or a black ass heifer. Never once was she ever concerned with how this made the girl feel. Angie would have her working like a slave when people came over. Most of these attacks were on days when Earl was not home so Tesha had to comply. Angie took it upon herself to degrade the girl every chance she got.

One day Tesha felt bold enough to try her aunt. Angie was having one of her fits and was taking her anger out on Tesha. They were in the front room and Earl was outside under the tree smoking and drinking, as usual. Angie was telling Tesha that she needed to clean her room because it was a mess.

"You are lazy as hell to lie in that dirty ass room

all day. It don't make no sense! That just go to show how nasty you are. I guess your crack head ass mama didn't teach you no better." She spat looking down her nose at the girl.

"Yes ma'am" was all Tesha could mumble out as she walked towards the front door.

Tesha hated when Angie talked about her mama like that. The way she belittled Chell, you would never think that they were blood sisters. Angie was always jealous of Chell. Even after turning to drugs, Chell still got all the attention because by then everyone wanted to save her. Chell was the first to have a child while Angie was barren. She was the first to get married, and although it didn't last long, she was married all the same. But that was no surprise considering her husband was strung out too. They both kept falling back onto drugs and then he eventually died from an overdose.

"Where the hell you think you're going?"

"Outside. I cleaned my room."

"I'll be the judge of that." Angie went to inspect Tesha's room just looking for something to fuss at her about.

"Tesha, you call this clean? Look at all that mess under your bed and falling out of the closet. You ain't going nowhere, clean it again. Matter of fact, clean the whole damn house too."

"Hell naw, you clean it!" Tesha surprised herself because she didn't mean for that to come out of her mouth.

"What did you say to me, wench?" Angie quizzed slowly walking towards Tesha.

"I...uh...nothing ma'am," she said slowly backing away from Angie.

"You talking back? Looks like I'm gonna have to teach you better. Go get a switch."

"I'm too big to get whipped."

"Oh, I see you the adult now, huh?" huffed Angie.

"No...I---"

Before she knew what happened, Angie slapped the taste out of Tesha's mouth. Tesha fell on the floor. Angie grabbed her by her hair and started dragging her into the front room. She snatched Tesha up off the floor and slapped her again sending her flying across the floor towards the wall. Tesha tried to fight back but Angie was too big and too strong for her to handle. Tesha kicked and screamed hoping that Earl would hear her and come save her. Angie started choking the girl down to the floor. Tesha thought she was going to black out, but then Angie released her. When she opened her eyes, Uncle Earl had Angie in a choke hold yelling for her to let the girl go.

"Angie, what is the matter with you?" Earl asked still holding her.

From the looks of it Earl was on her back tying to hold her back. Angie was like a wild bull, and Earl was her cowboy.

"Let me go," Angie said through clenched teeth.

"Not until you calm down."

Angie gave in after a few more minutes of struggling to get free. Tesha was pulling herself up off the floor and sat on the sofa holding her now bruising neck crying all the while. Angie stormed out of the house and took off. That would be the first and the last time Tesha rose up against her aunt because she knew that if it weren't for Earl, Angie would have killed her.

"What happened Tesha?"

"Auntie just snapped on me."

"For no reason?" he quizzed.

"Well, I did get smart with her a lil."

"A lil, huh?"

"What happened to you telling her never to touch me again?" Tesha asked rubbing her neck.

"I didn't tell you to go askin' for an ass whoopin." Earl stated whipping sweat from his brow.

Angie hated that little bitch. She knew that she was wrong, but she didn't care. There was no other way for her to express her hatred for her niece. She knew that she would have to deal with Earl later, but she didn't care. Whatever it took to keep her man, she was going to do. In her mind, the fight with Tesha was long overdue. Angie felt that Tesha was the other woman that she had to endure for the sake of her relationship. She was determined to find a way to get rid of Tesha, and if it weren't for going to prison and losing him all together, she probably would just take her ass out.

It's Over Now

When I agreed to take Tesha in, I had no idea how much she would remind me of Chell. It's like all the anger I felt for Chell over the years has transferred to Tesha. I have to remind myself that she is only a child and does not really understand what she is doing to me. I hoped that after a while, I would dismiss all those crazy thoughts. But when I see them together, I have to force myself to believe that there is nothing weird going on. She just chooses to stick close to Earl because he lets her get away with murder.

Without even knowing what was going on yesterday, Earl took her side again. I am getting sick and tired of that shit. Every time I turn around, she's running to Earl. And the killing part is that he protects her like she his daughter or something. It eats me up inside that I've become jealous of their relationship. But I also see all the stares when we are out in public. My family is always talking about them and how Tesha is always right up under his ass. When I bring this to his attention, he says that I'm the crazy one. It is really hard for me sometimes. I know he wanted kids, but that is something that I cannot help. We had tried for years. Outside of the one I lost in Vegas, nothing. I don't care what the doctors say; I know that God will bless me with a baby because I'm a good Christian.

I still have an image to uphold, and Tesha is not going to get away with this shit. Damn, I aint got no more minutes on my phone and I need to call up to Bolingbrook. I guess I'll run over to my cousin's house so that I can call Chell. Hell, I'm down here raising her child while she up in there with her new husband living it up. I haven't even got husband number one, and here she is on number two. I hear that this one has some money, so it is high time Chell played mama for a while so I can work on my own man. Maybe with Tesha gone, Earl will see how much he loves me again and marry me this time, for real. Our last attempt was a big waste of time and my money.

After about an hour of convincing Angie had achieved her goal. Chell was a bit reluctant to have Tesha come stay with her, but she knew she needed to do the right thing by her. After some coaxing,

she agreed and everything was set for next Friday--
the quicker the better. Now all Angie had to do was
convince Earl that this is a good idea and a good
time to start working on getting her relationship
back on track.

MANY RIVERS TO CROSS

"How was your flight baby?" Chell asked nervously.

It had been 3 years since Chell had seen Tesha and over a decade since she had to care for her. Things had not been easy for her, but now that she had Enoch, her life was looking up. Deep down she regretted not being there for Tesha, but what can you do about the past? Today was a new day, and Chell was set on mending the broken relationship between her and her daughter.

"I'm okay ma, where is Enoch?"

"He had to work baby girl, so it's just you and me," Chell added with a half smile. Chell was really nervous about this visit, and she wanted everything to run smoothly and maybe then Tesha would want to stay.

"Can we go get something to eat?" Tesha asked rubbing her belly for emphases. "I'm starving."

"I thought I would cook you a nice dinner because I know your aunt can't cook to save her life," Chell said through a heartfelt giggle.

Chell was right; Angie was not the best cook in the world. She tried, but the only thing that was really eatable was her macaroni and cheese. Her cooking was not too bad; it just wasn't on par with the rest of the family. The Andersons prided themselves on being some of the best cooks in their small town. Even the men could burn. This was mainly because they were a female dominated family, and the boys had to learn to fend for themselves. Every year they would have a cook-off during their family reunion where every family had to contribute a dish. The elders served as the judges. Whoever won received the family trophy and bragging rights for the year. Needless to say, Angie could kiss getting that trophy goodbye.

"That will be fine, just keep it light 'cause I have to keep my figure tight," Tesha said with a sway of her tiny hips.

If my mama think I'm gonna stay up here, she got another thing coming. I know Aunt Angie wanted me out of her house, but I can't believe that Uncle Earl went along with it. Last time she tried to send me away, he let her know quick, fast, and in a hurry that if I go, she go. All this "we need to bond" shit is a waste of time.

Chell ain't never been a mama to me. Come to think of it, neither has Angie, but at least she was there. All my life, my so-called mama was getting high. There were no happy birthdays, Christmases, or even mid-night refrigerator raids. I can't even remember the last time my mother told me that she loved me. It has always been about her and her drugs. My daddy played a small part in my life when I was younger, but I haven't seen him in a few years. He used to buy me stuff all the time and take me to the movies, but when he got married and had another daughter, I got lost in the mix. Well to hell with sitting by the sidelines. I'm 16 now and I have a man of my own, who loves me. This little trip is just a minor setback, but I will fix that. Tesha thought.

Oh hell! This is going to be a long visit because I can see now that I'm going to have to knock her little ass down a peg or two. Group taught me that I have to have patience with family members that suffered the side effects of my addiction. Patience I have but tolerance for fast ass little girls I don't have. Who does she think the she is anyway? Ass ain't big as a gnat and got the nerve to try and twist her tail. When I get her all settled in, I will lay down the rules because I don't want any misunderstandings about who is the adult here. Chell thought to herself.

It wasn't long before Chell started to see some things in her daughter that she did not like. It was time to talk to her sister.

"Angie, why didn't you tell me that Tesha was so hot?" Chell asked Angie while shifting the phone's receiver to her other ear.

"What are you talking about, Chell?" Angie quizzed, honestly surprised because Tesha was always at home with her and Earl. She never talked about boys in that way. Hell, she hadn't even been on her first date.

"Girl please, Tesha running around here like some little slut."

"What happened?"

"Where should I start? First off, she has been skipping school with May's baby girl Tangy. I found a movie stub from a show over in Hyde Park during school hours. She has been sneaking out at night. And to top it all off, last night I woke up because I thought I heard something downstairs. I go down there and when I didn't see anything, I went to check on her on my way back to bed and guess what? This little heifer had a boy or should I say a grown man in her bed."

"What were they doing, girl?" Angie asked with too much enjoyment for Chell's taste.

"Girl, I don't even want to say. But what I will

say is that they looked like they had seen a ghost when I flipped on the light. Now when I think of it it's kinda of funny. Angie, when I tell you that dude jumped up and out the window in one swoop, you would have thought it was a scene from an action flick. Tesha couldn't say one word because she was cold busted."

"Well, what you gone do with her?"

"Gone do…done already done is more like it. I beat that ass like she stole something. How dare she disrespect my home?"

"That's what she needed all along," Angie said feeling a little victory in Tesha's punishment. She wished that she would have been beating her ass a long time ago, but no, Earl didn't think it was right to beat a child.

"I put her tail on punishment until after school is out for Spring Break. I don't give a damn if she looks at them walls until she graduates."

"Good luck with your daughter, Chell. I didn't know that she could be such a handful."

This was not all true. Angie never experienced such behavior from Tesha, but she knew deep down that the apple didn't fall too far from the tree. Chell had boys sneaking in and out of the window when mama went to work all time. Mama used to beat her ass all the time because she was too fast, but I guess that now that she had found Jesus, she somehow forgot all about that.

"Speaking of Spring Break, how about letting Tesha come here for a visit?" Angie asked hoping she would say no.

"Why? I thought you were glad that she was gone. Besides, it's only been a few months."

"Yeah, I know, but we miss her a little. Plus, this will give you a little break, and maybe I can get Earl to talk some sense into her. She always listens to him."

The truth of the matter is that Earl told her that Tesha needs to come back home. He says that when he talks to her, all she does is complain about being away and how much she misses her friends and wants to come back. His complaining outweighs Tesha's though. Angie is getting tired of hearing about how this is all her fault and how Tesha didn't need to go in the first place. To add insult to injury, Earl warned her that if something happens to Tesha up there, he would never forgive her.

"Okay, she can come, but she has to be back in 2 weeks for school on Monday morning," Chell warned.

Angie thought it was funny hearing her sounding like a real mother.

Don't Kill My Vibe

*T*esha and Earl were in hog heaven for these past few days. Angie didn't bother them much because business had picked up in her salon, which was really a converted storage shed, but it worked all the same. Earl really enjoyed having Tesha back home. They would go fishing, hunting, and hang out under the tree. In the late afternoons, they would lounge around all day talking and drinking. By now, this was such a regular event around Maplesville that no one even bothered to care anymore.

One lazy afternoon, Earl asked Tesha how she was enjoying Bolingbrook. His plan was to get her to see how much she was missed so that she would want to come back home to him.

"So how you makin' out up there?" asked Earl in between sips.

"It's alright, but I wish I was here instead. My mom doesn't let me do nothing!" she whined.

"See, that's what I used to tell you…ain't nobody gonna love you like we do. See, she thinks that going to school and church is all you can do with yourself. You're a young lady who needs to be out enjoying life, not stuck up in the house."

"I want to come back Uncle Earl."

"Well, you know Angie ain't tryna hear that. We're gonna have to think of something to convince her."

"Like what?" asked Tesha.

"I don't know yet. How are they treating you up there? Is Chell using again?" asked Earl tying to come up with a scheme.

"Naw, she is real clean and her and Enoch take good care of me. He real nice, but he tries too hard to be my friend tho."

Just then it dawned on Earl.

"How nice *is* he?"

"I don't know. He is just always asking me if I need anything…if I want anything…do I want to watch a movie or something."

"Well, you know if he gets too friendly, you better let me know. Angie and I will be on the first thing smoking to come and get you."

Tesha was way ahead of Earl, her wheels already turning. She knew how to get back home; all she needed now was opportunity.

Those two weeks in Maplesville were heavenly for Tesha. She was back in her own bed and hanging out with Earl. She enjoyed being out of school and being able to do whatever she wanted to do. Tesha was not looking forward to going back to Bolingbrook…at…all. Every time someone asked her if she was ready to go back to Chell, she lied and said yeah.

When Tesha's cousin Ella asked her about going back to Bolingbrook, she decided to tell the truth. She figured that since Ella had never been one to get all up in her business and tell her what to do, the truth would be just fine.

Ella was Tesha's second cousin and she had just moved to Maplesville when she got out of the military. Ella had been gone for over 10 years and since her return, she has pretty much kept to herself. She works and goes to school so she didn't spend too much time with the rest of the clan. Now, this didn't stop information from coming to her. The situation between Earl and Tesha had made it way around the world to Ella while she was still overseas. She didn't want to get involved with the family gossip. Plus, she didn't believe it.

"When does school start Tesha?" asked Ella.

"Monday."

"You ready to go back?"

"Nope. I'll be back in a few weeks."

"How? You will be in school." Ella said with a confused look on her face.

"You'll see. I don't wanna be up there. I want to be right here."

"Why? You have a chance to experience new things and develop a relationship with your mother."

"Ella, I want to be here with Aunt Angie and Uncle Earl; it's fun here."

"Cut the shit, Tesha! What's going on with you and Earl?" Ella asked tired of hearing the gossip and wanting the truth.

"Hahaha, what chu talking about Ella? Ain't nothing going on with me and Uncle Earl; he's cool people."

"Um hum. If something is going on over there, you need to tell somebody and get some help. I'll help you." Ella was being really sincere with Tesha, but it was falling on deaf ears. Tesha's mind was made up.

"Ella, I promise you that nothing is going on."

Ella knew that Tesha was lying because of that sheepish grin plastered across her face. What she couldn't understand was why. If Earl was messing with her, why would she *want* to come back? Then it dawned on her…Stockholm syndrome. Ella had just gone over this in her behavioral science class. This was worse than Ella could have imagined. While she was away in the military she has heard a lot of horrible things and she knew that she would have to talk to Angie about this, but Lord knows that it won't be pleasant.

The next day Ella invited Angie over for dessert. Ella was a great cook who was always experimenting with new foods, and since Angie liked to eat, it was a perfect icebreaker.

"Hey, Chic! What's smelling so good?" asked Angie as she entered Ella's home.

"Hey Girly-girl. I'm in the kitchen, Come on back."

Ella had baked a homemade apple pie with a buttery pecan crust. This was all for Angie because she knew she would love it. Ella fixed Angie a slice and topped it with a scoop of homemade vanilla ice cream. Ella didn't eat baked fruit, so she only had some ice cream.

"How has it been with Tesha back? She told me that she wanted to stay."

"Yeah, I know she does. She ain't feeling Chell and all her rules too much," Angie said in between bites.

"You could be right, but don't you think she

needs that discipline?"

"Yeah, but sometimes Chell can be extra."

"I guess so. There was something I wanted to ask you about Tesha and Earl." Ella figured that she had no choice but to just jump right into it.

"Oh yeah…what?" Angie quizzed giving Ella a side-eye glance.

"Is something going on with them two Angie? I mean, they really do spend a lot of time together."

"Oh here you go. I can't believe you would ask me that, Ella."

"I know, Angie. I usually stay out of other folk's business, but this is serious. I think Tesha has Stockholm syndrome."

"What the hell is that?"

"It is a mental condition where someone who has been abused starts to develop an emotional bond with their abuser; they see nothing wrong with what is happening to them. They even become protective of their abuser, and in some cases they can even fall in love with them. It's not her fault, it's a survival technique."

"You have been reading too many of them damn psychology books." *Just then it dawned on her what Ella was trying to do; she was just like everybody else.* "Just 'cause you in school for the shit don't mean you can try to mind fuck me!" Angie shouted.

"Angie, I'm not trying to mess with your mind. I'm trying to understand what is going on here."

"Look Ella, don't nobody help me take care of Tesha but Earl. When Tesha told me that Earl touched her when she was younger, I did what I thought I was supposed to do. I put his black ass out and took her to the doctor. They said nothing had happened to her. When I got back home, they both are singing the same tune that "nothing happened". The police can't do nothing because she said she was lying and nothing happened. Plus, there was no evidence of any sex. What am I supposed to do? Besides, nobody did anything when it was happening to us."

"To who? What happened, Angie?" Ella had no idea what Angie was talking about. Plus, that was the dumbest shit she had ever heard. If something had happened to Angie why would she let it happen to Tesha?

"Nothing, Ella. Just leave it alone. Thanks for the pie, but you need to stick to minding your own damned business."

With that, Angie was out the door.

WICKED GAMES

Back at Chell's, things were different. Unlike her sister, Chell was pleasant, and what she learned in church, she applied to her life daily. There was not too much cursing in her home, no name calling, no belittling, and most of all, no violence. On the other hand, Chell and Angie were a lot alike-- neither of them took any mess. Chell made sure Tesha had everything she needed from clothes to money. But with these luxuries, Tesha had to pull her weight. Tesha had daily chores, and she was required to maintain no less than a B average in school. The academic part was no problem because Tesha was a bright girl if she applied herself, but doing chores became more of an issue every day.

Tesha knew that her mother was a stickler on having and keeping a clean house. So she decided that this is where she would start slacking off first, in hopes of being sent back to Earl. As the weeks passed, Tesha and Chell had constant arguments about the tidiness of their home. Tesha gave in after being bitten by ants one night; she decided that being nasty was not as pleasing as she had hoped. One night while lying awake trying to think of a new scheme to change her situation, she thought about her conversation with Earl under the tree. Then, like a light bulb, it came to her. From her own experiences, the best way to get a child removed from a home is to bring up accusations of abuse. She knew that physical abuse was out of the question because she had no bruises to show, and no one in the family would believe her without evidence. Plus, ass-whooping in a black family was a part of life. If you do something wrong, you get a whooping-- it's just that simple. As long as there were no bruises or broken bones, most families considered this a normal form of punishment. Her claims had to be something that was unacceptable in any household. It didn't take long for Tesha to come up with a new plan.

Tesha waited until her mother had the night shift at the hospital before she made her move. This particular evening, it was raining, and a huge thunder storm was brewing. At around midnight, Tesha sprang into action. She knew that Enoch was in a dead sleep because he had taken some cold medicine before he went to bed. The lightening was flashing every few minutes, and the thunder was cracking and breaking the silence of night. Tesha put on her night gown and grabbed a pair of panties. She crept down the hall to her mother's room, pausing every few steps to calm her nerves.

On the other side of the bedroom door, Tesha could hear Enoch snoring. She paused as she grabbed the door knob. *This is it, no turning back.* She slowly entered the master suite and went over to her mom's vanity table. Tesha put a few drops of Chell's favorite fragrance behind her ears and on her inner thigh as she had seen her mom do many times. As quietly as possible, Tesha climbed into bed beside Enoch. Every time the thunder would crack, she would move closer to him until she was nose to nose with her mother's husband. Tesha reached underneath the comforter and found Enoch's manhood. She slowly slid her hands inside the opening of his boxer shorts and started to massage him. In no time Enoch's body started to respond to her touch. Enoch moaned as he reached for who he thought was his wife. In the darkness Enoch could not see anything, but he could smell his beautiful wife which turned him on. As the thunder cracked, Tesha gripped him harder; her lessons with Earl were paying off.

Enoch reached for Tesha's breast, but she stopped him and moved his hands to her butt. Him touching her breast would have been a dead giveaway since Chell was at least two cup sizes larger. Other than that, the two were almost identical. Tesha was giving Enoch the best hand job he ever had. Just as he was about to explode, lightening struck and his wife transformed into her daughter right before his eyes. It took a second or Earl to realize what had just happened. Could his eyes be playing tricks on him, or was he actually in bed with his wife's daughter? Enoch jumped from the bed and backed up against the wall. All he could say was "What have I done?" A sudden coolness drifted into the room and brushed pass Enoch, its breeze brought his attention to his swollen, exposed manhood. As he tried to cover himself with one of the decorative pillows, Tesha got up and started walking towards him. Enoch slipped into the bathroom and locked the door. Enoch yelled through the door for Tesha to get out of his room over and over. Tesha stood there in horror as the realization of what she had just done set in. She ran from the room slamming the door behind her.

After about 15 minutes in the bathroom praying that this was a nightmare, Enoch cautiously stepped out into what was once his and his wife's private oasis. After surveying the room and finding no traces of Tesha, Enoch locked the door and climbed back into bed trying to think of how he was going to tell his wife that her daughter was in bed with him.

At 8 am the next morning, Chell came home from a long night of caring for her patients. She had just received her nursing license last year and was working swing shift at the hospital. All she wanted to do when she got home was to climb into bed next to her husband.

Tesha was already up and gone to school, so it was peaceful. Chell expected to see her husband in the kitchen making breakfast because he didn't have to be at work until 9. But as she looked around her spacious kitchen, there was no Enoch. She called to him but got no answer. Chell figured that he must have gone in early.

In her room, Chell ran her some bath water so that she could soak her tension away. With her working nights these past two weeks and Tesha being home all the time, Chell and Enoch rarely had any private time. Her body needed him in the worst way. Next week she would be back on days, and they had a lot of making up to do. The thought brought a smile to Chell's face as she started to undress.

"Will Enoch ever learn to make up a bed?" Chell asked herself aloud as she saw the mess her husband made in his haste to leave the house. The covers were balled up and pillows were thrown on the floor.

Being the neat freak that she is, Chell began to tidy up her room because she could not sleep in a nasty space. As she pulled the covers off her king size sleigh bed, a balled up piece of red lace popped out and landed at her feet. Chell inspected the material, not sure of what it was until she unfolded it. Chell was shocked to see the panties. It was as if someone had hit her in the chest because all of a sudden she could not breathe. She sat on the edge of her bed looking at the undergarments with all sorts of visions going through her head.

Whose could these be? They're not mine. Is Enoch cheating on me? In my own home...my own bed? How could he do this to us? For what seemed like forever, Chell sat on her bed and cried tears of a broken hearted woman. After the tears subsided, she just sat there staring off into the distance. The tub started to overflow and the warm water on her feet broke Chell out of her zombie-like state. Chell walked into the bathroom to turn off what was going to be a peaceful bath and let the water out. Chell called out sick to work that evening because she knew that she could not tend to the needs of others if she was not in the right state of mind. Thoughts of their beginning flashed before her as she sat in disbelief.

From the first day they met in the grocery store, they have been inseparable. Enoch worked for the city's utility department. He had been a supervisor there for the past 5 years and had great hopes of becoming part of the management team. Enoch really was a good man. When he met Chell 4 years ago, he was a single father of two-- a 17-year-old son and a 15-year-old daughter. He and Chell hit it off right away. He didn't look at Chell any differently when she confessed to him her darkest secrets of being on drugs and losing her kids. In fact, he had a confession of his own. At the time that they met, he had been 7 years clean of alcoholism. After his children's mother died tragically in a car accident, he turned to the bottle. When the state threatened to take his babies away, he got his life together. Enoch knew that he would just die if he lost them too. The kids took to Chell right from the gate; they liked her a lot and were glad that she had met their father. A year after the kids left the nest; they decided to make it official. Chell and Enoch had a very traditional wedding, white dress and honeymoon included. For the past 3 years, life for the Newton's was good.

The past few years with Enoch had been great. They loved each other so much, and Chell couldn't help but wonder when and what had changed for him. Enoch never let on that he was not happy with their life. What had she done to cause him to stray was all that Chell could think about. The weight of the day's events was heavy on Chell's shoulders. Her mind was going in a million different directions at once. Chell went downstairs, and as she walked through their home, moments that they shared came to mind. Thoughts of when they first moved in and all the work they had put into this HUD home to turn it into their dream house.

Their house sat in a cul-de-sac of a quaint subdivision. It was a two-story, three bedrooms, 2 ½ bathroom mess until they transformed it into the immaculate, eye-catching place they called home. They both took 2 weeks off of work after they closed on their home so they could redecorate their castle. Those two fixed and touched-up everything in that home from the pipes to the finishing paint job. Their home was unique, and for the past 2 years, they have had the best yard in their neighborhood. But now, none of that mattered because all that Chell can see is that broke down shell of a house they purchased for 40K on that cool autumn day in September.

She could not bring herself to sleep in their bedroom so she took a nap on the living room sofa. The ringing of the telephone woke Chell from her slumber. It was Tesha calling to see if she could stay the night at her cousin's house. Chell agreed because she preferred to talk to Enoch without Tesha present. Just then, the front door opened and there stood Enoch. The look of Chell half sitting on the sofa still in her uniform with a tear-streaked face told him that Tesha must have told her what happened. His guilt-ridden face confirmed her suspensions.

BAD ROMANCE

"Hey baby, how was your day?" Enoch asked still standing in the doorway.

Chell didn't realize how long she had been asleep, but the darkness outside said that night had fallen.

"Good, and yours?" Chell asked sitting up and taking a long stretch.

"It was a rough one, baby. I think I'm just gonna head up to bed."

"Wait a minute, baby; I want to talk to you," Chell said motioning for Enoch to come and sit next to her.

"Can it wait until I get out of the shower?" Enoch asked stalling for time.

"Actually, it can't."

With that tone in her voice, Enoch knew that Chell meant business. Chell tried to steady her mind so that she could get the truth from her husband. She figured that if she kept her cool, Enoch would be more forthcoming. If he tried to lie, she would show him her evidence.

"Enoch, I'm not going to beat around the bush. Are you cheating on me?"

"No, baby, I would never do that to us. Why would you think such a thing?" Enoch figured that he would turn the question so that he could know how much Chell knew.

"All you have to do is tell me the truth. Have you found someone more desirable?"

"No, baby, I love you and you know that you are the only woman for me," he said still standing in the doorway. Truth is, Enoch was afraid to get too close to her.

"Look Enoch, I know that you had a woman in my bed last night so stop the fucking lying to me!" Chell could not control her emotions any longer. The tears started to flow, and Enoch felt like shit. He thought about telling her a lie, but he knew that from all that they went through, she deserved better.

"Baby, I am going to tell you the truth, but I want you to hear me out before you say anything, okay?"

Chell nodded, took in a deep breath and slowly exhaled as to brace for shock.

"Do you remember last night when I got home that I was congested and had a fever? Well after you left for work, I took me some cold medicine and you know how that stuff knocks me out. Anyway, sometime during the night I was awakened by someone massaging me down there." *Enoch pointed to his pelvic area.* Baby, I swear that I thought it was you tryna get a little freaky, you know how you do sometimes. Bay, remember that time we went to the park and you put your hand in my—"

"Get back to the matter at hand Enoch." Chell was visibly irritated with his attempt to make this a joking matter.

"Anyway, I was half sleep and still feeling the effects of the cold medicine. I honestly thought it was you. Baby, you got to believe me; I would never cheat on you." Fighting back tears, Enoch walked across the room and knelt down in front of Chell. She could see the sincerity in his eyes, and she wanted to believe that he was not lying. But whose panties were in her bed?

"How could you think it was me when you know that I was at work?"

"I didn't know what time it was…I thought that it was morning and that you were back home."

"Couldn't you tell the difference?"

"Baby, it was dark in the room, and I never

opened my eyes. I just smelled you and thought it was you."

"What do you mean you smelled me?" Chell asked sounding confused.

"It was your perfume; you know…the one I like. You're the only one I know who wears it… who else could it have been?"

"Enoch, I found these panties, and I want to know who they belong to." Holding up her findings, Chell was pissed all over again.

"Chell, those must belong to Tesha," Enoch said letting the tears flow. He knew how this sounded, but he could not lie to his wife.

"Tesha?" Chell jumped to her feet. It was like Enoch's words burned her soul.

Chell paced across the room, and her pain was evident. Her sobs were loud and screechy. Had the man that she loved molested her baby girl? How could he? Chell's mind went wild. She lunged at Enoch with all her might, hitting and cursing him for being a child molester. Enoch tried to block her blows. He would never strike her. He took it because he could only imagine how she must have felt because if someone had touched his daughter, he would try to kill them too.

"Baby, wait! I didn't touch her. You can ask her, she'll tell you I didn't. Go on ask-er!" Enoch yelled above Chell's wails for Tesha but received no answer.

"She's not here. She's staying the weekend at May's house. What do you mean you didn't touch her? She was in bed with you and left her panties behind. What else could have been going on?"

"Chell, I swear on my mama's grave that I didn't touch her; you gotta believe me. Like I said, I woke up with her touching me. It was storming out, so when the lightning flashed, I saw that it was not you, and I damn near jumped out of my skin! I jumped out of bed and ran into the bathroom. I yelled at her to get out of our room, and I stayed in that bathroom until I heard her leave. She must have left them in the bed or something. Baby, I swear to God that I...DID...NOT...TOUCH... HER!"

As crazy as his story sounded, she could not help but feel that he was telling the truth. There was only one way to get to the bottom of this and that was to talk to Tesha.

"Enoch, I don't know what to think right now, and I need some space." Chell's tears had subsided, and her mind was confused. *Could this be Tesha's fault? Or is Enoch trying to cover his ass?*

"Baby, you want me to get you something?" Enoch said rising from his spot on the sofa and heading towards the kitchen.

"No. I just need some space to think. Your bags are in the closet." Chell walked towards the stairs. She had packed his bags earlier and was ready to send his tail walking.

"My bags? Ooh baby, baby, please don't put me out." Enoch ran over to Chell and tried to stop her from going upstairs. She kept walking. He hit the floor with a thud.

"Chell, I can't live without you. Don't do this," he begged. He knew that he could not live without her, but he also knew that she needed some space. Enoch had to man up. He reluctantly retrieved his bags from the closet and walked back out to his truck in the pouring rain.

UNPRETTY

*D*amn that Tesha. I can't believe I let myself get into that position. How could she do this to her own mother? I know Chell has not always been there, but she was in no position to raise a child. She made sure that Tesha was in a good home with her sister, and that was better than nothing. I would never touch a child in that manner; hell, I have my own children. I have never done anything like that to them, so why on earth would I do that to someone else's baby? I knew that girl was trouble the moment she arrived at our door step. But I tried to be supportive of Chell and her decisions. She needed to have a relationship with her daughter, but not at my expense. I have to get to the bottom of this and clear my good name.

Enoch pulled up in front of his sister May's house. Chell had said that Tesha was staying the night there. He knew that he had to confront

Tesha and get this mess straight before it went any further.

"Hold on, I'm coming!" shouted May as she shuffled to her front door.

Enoch recognized that as the voice of his younger sister Mayla, May for short. He was hoping that he wouldn't have to explain anything to her. He was hoping to read her expression; it would give him clues as to how much Tesha had revealed.

"Hey Love, what brings you around my way?" May questioned. She was only accustomed to seeing her older brother on Sundays for their family dinner, so this was a bit of a surprise.

"I came to see Tesha for a sec. I need to ask her something," he said trying to sound carefree.

"You coulda just called; we do have a phone," May joked.

"Yeah, I know. But I was on my way out and just decided to stop by. Can you call her for me?" Enoch backed out the door without another word. The look on his face told May that this was not really a social call, so she did as he requested. Within a few minutes, Tesha emerged from the house with a smile on her face wearing her pajamas.

"We need to talk," spat Enoch.

"About what E--?"

"You know good and well what. Why were

you in my bed last night? Your mother knows. She thought I was cheating on her; then she thought I was molesting you. I need you to tell her the truth."

"Oh...um...I don't think I can help you E."

"What?"

"I mean you did try to molest me. That's why I ran out of the room and didn't come home tonight."

"You got to be joking," Enoch said in pure disbelief.

"Sorry," Tesha said as she started back into the house.

Enoch was beside himself. He grabbed her frail arm and spun her around to face him not wanting to hurt her, but he did want to get his point across.

"You will not tell her such lies; it will kill her, and you know it. You need to stop playing these damned games and tell your mother the truth."

Just then, the front door opened and there stood May with a look of disgust on her face.

"Enoch! Turn that baby loose," she spat at him, rushing over to Tesha's aid.

"Not until she tells the truth, May!"

"Chell just called me. Tell me what she said wasn't true, Enoch," May said in disbelief.

"It is, but it is not what you think. Tesha started this and she is going to finish it by telling you both the truth."

With that, Tesha went into one of the best per-formances either of them had seen live. She started crying hysterically and flopping around trying to get out of Enoch's death grip. She started yelling so loudly that lights started popping on in the neigh-boring homes. Enoch turned her loose so that no peeping eyes would call the law. But he wanted to shake the shit out of her lying ass.

"Help me, Auntie May. He is trying to hurt me again," cried Tesha as she turned to May and wrapped her arms around her thick waist.

May pulled Tesha close in an effort to protect her. "Baby, what's going on?"

"Auntie May, he tried to rape me last night while Mama was at work!" she blurted through tears.

Enoch almost fell off the porch at this outright lie. He could not believe his ears.

"Brother, please tell me you didn't?" May asked through her tears.

"Mayla, you know me better that that. I would never do anything so horrible.

"Tesha, why are you telling these foul lies on me? What did I ever do to you?" Enoch asked al-most in tears.

His spirits were crushed, and he could not wrap his mind around a reason behind this dilemma.

May pulled Tesha inside and told Enoch that he better leave or she would call the police. If Enoch didn't know any better, he could have sworn that Tesha smiled at him as he was leaving.

As Enoch drove to a nearby motel, he could not believe what was happening to his life. How could his world come crashing down in less than 24 hours? *I go to church, I pray, I pay my tithes. Lord, what is going on? I know that I'm not supposed to question your doings, but Lord why has thou forsaken me? Father, you know that I have never done anything to that girl but try to be a positive male figure in her life. Father God, I pray to you that you will make this right. Lord, please help me.*

Enoch prayed the whole ride to the motel. He was lost.

Situation #9

*T*hat was easier than I thought it would be. I didn't even have to say too much. I almost decided against this whole set up, but that fool had to open his mouth. Mama should have put his simple ass out. He had to know that it was not her in bed with him. I'm sure that my bougie ass mama don't know nothin' about jacking a man off.

Now I have to shift my plan into overdrive. I didn't really want to bring anyone else in to this mess, but May just fell into it. I know that May is gonna want to talk to me, but she already knows too much now. I am not giving her any details.

"Tesha, baby do you want to tell your Auntie May what happened last night?" Concern was all in May's voice.

"Not really, Auntie. I just want to forget it all like it was a bad dream," Tesha said sounding like an innocent child instead of the conniving person she really was.

"You sure? I just wanna help you sweetie."

"I know Auntie, I just wanna go to bed now, okay?"

I'ma call my Mama in the morning to give her my version of what happened. I've got it all rehearsed. I was in my room minding my business when Enoch called me up to their room. I walked in, and he just jumped on me. I tried to fight him off, but he was too strong. Since I only had on my night gown, he threw me on the bed and snatched my panties off. During the struggle, I managed to knee him in the nuts and that gave me enough time to get up out of there. I was so scared that I didn't want to come home after school. Yeah, that's about it. I think I covered all my bases. I'll be back in Maplesville by the end of the week, Tesha thought to herself.

First thing in the morning, she called Chell but I got no answer. Tesha knew that she would have to face her sooner or later, so she told May that she was going home to be with her mother. She bought it without any further questions. Tesha told May that she would call her if she needed her and to tell Tangy that she would call her later.

Chell rose this morning as stiff as a board. She never slept on the sofa, but this time she had no choice. She could not bring herself to get back into that tainted bed and it had to go as soon as possible. Just the thought of what happened in that bed made her sick to her stomach. She had not heard from Enoch since she put him out. It was Saturday and Tesha was still at May's, so the house was empty.

An inner voice told Chell to get herself together. Whatever happened was not her fault, so wallowing in self-pity was not an option. She got up from the sofa and took a shower in hopes to wash away some of the tension her body was under. She wasn't in the mood for conversation, so she turned the ringers on the phones off and went about her business of cleaning her house. Cleaning to some was a punishment, but Chell looked at cleaning as a form of therapy. It always helped her to clear her mind. She went into the den and pulled out all her gospel CD's. After searching and finding her favorite various artists CD, she popped it into their stereo system and turned up the volume way past a suitable level.

During her therapy session, Chell cleaned her home from top to bottom. Starting on the first floor and working her way up. When she came to her bedroom, she paused and decided against entering. Instead, she went to her daughter's room which was on the other side of the hallway. As she stood in the doorway taking a mental picture of Tesha's space, she noticed that nothing was in its place. *How many times do I have to tell this girl to clean her room?* Chell tackled the pigsty that used to be her arts and crafts room. Every time she picked up an item of clothing, it was like another magically appeared in its place. She could not imagine how this girl lived in here.

Chell took the broom and swept everything from under the bed in one motion. She looked to make sure she got everything, and a piece of material was left untouched back against the wall. In order to retrieve it, she had to pull the bed away from the wall. *I'll do that last.*

Chell worked for over an hour in Tesha's room before she was satisfied with the end product. As she was putting the finishing touches on the room with sprits of clean linen spray, she remembered the cloth behind the bed. Chell pushed the bed away from the wall, got the cloth and noticed that it smelled familiar.

She held the garment up to the light to see it better. It was a sexy gown. It couldn't have been Tesha's, it was too grown up. After a closer look at the garment, Chell realized that it was her lingerie; she got it as a wedding gift but hadn't worn it in years. She threw the gown in the hamper along with all the other dirty clothes Tesha had sprawled about the room and headed to the laundry room. As she walked, the cool breeze from her pace stirred up the scent on the gown. Then it hit her. *My perfume.* She dropped the basket and pulled out the gown again and sniffed it. This *is* my perfume. Chell ran upstairs and into her room. She searched her vanity for her fragrance, and it was not where she left it. Chell kept all her perfumes stored in the slide drawers on her vanity table because there were too many to sit up top. She searched each drawer -- still nothing. She stepped back, and there it was on the floor next to the trash can. Chell knew good and well that she had not worn that scent recently. This was not an everyday fragrance. It was called *Mimosa,* and it was fairly expensive and very hard to find. Just then, she realized that this is why Enoch had smelled her. His story was adding up. But why would Tesha have on her perfume? She knew that I didn't allow her to wear it. This mess is getting odder by the second. I need to talk to Tesha now.

Just then, Tesha walked through the front door. "Mommy, I need to talk to you."

"I was thinking the same thing," Chell stated with a stern look on her face.

The two went into the dining room and sat at the table. Tesha wanted to make her performance as heartfelt as possible so that Chell would buy it. She took a few breaths to calm her nerves before she began to lay down her lies. After she was finished, Chell just looked at her. Tesha admitted to taking the gown from the room a few days ago but said nothing of wearing her perfume.

"Tesha, did Enoch say anything to you when you walked into the room?" Chell asked quizzing her daughter.

"No, Mama, he didn't say one word."

"Had you been in my room earlier after I left for work?"

"No, Mama. I know that you don't like people going in your bedroom."

"Where are the panties that you had on so that we can take them to the police?"

"The police? Mama, do we have to call the police? I mean, I wasn't hurt or anything. He didn't hurt me, Mama." Fear took over Tesha's mind.

This surprised Chell because she knew that a crime of this magnitude needed to be reported. She figured that Tesha would want to have Enoch reported and prosecuted for his crimes. But to her surprise, Tesha was adamant about not reporting Enoch.

"But baby don't you think he should go to jail for what he tried to do to you?"

"He didn't hurt me, Mama. I just don't think that I can stay here with him here anymore."

"Where would you go, Tesha? I think you need to be here with me."

"Well, here with you is what got me in this mess." The words came out before she could catch them. They stung Chell like a slap. Could Tesha be actually blaming her for what happened?

"Mama, I can go back to Maplesville with Auntie Angie," she said hopeful that her plan was working.

Just then, the front door swung open and in stormed Enoch. The sudden burst of energy interrupted Chell and Tesha's conversation. The look on Enoch's face told Tesha that she was in big trouble, so she had to think fast. She got up and ran around the table so that Chell could shield her.

"Chell, this is going to end right here and right now. I did not touch Tesha, and she is going to tell you the truth." Enoch was not trying to hear anything but the truth, and he was prepared to defend his name to the bitter end.

"Mama, he is lying. He did try to rape me last night!" Tesha yelled and pointed towards Enoch.

At this point, Chell didn't know who to believe because she loved them both.

"Tesha, tell your mama that you came in *my* room and got in *my* bed on your own."

"I didn't. You called me into your room, and I was just seeing what you wanted when you attacked me."

"I did no sucha thang, and you know it," Enoch said getting madder by the second.

Chell stood up waving her hands so that they both would be quiet. She stepped away from them both and stopped mid stride. Chell turned to face her husband and her baby girl with fresh tears in her eyes.

"Enoch, did you try to rape my daughter?"

"No, I did not," Enoch said with conviction.

"Tesha, did you make a move on Enoch?"

"No, Mama, I would not do that to you."

"Well, one of you is lying, and we are not leaving until I get the truth," Chell announced with folded arms, and she went to sit back in her seat at the table. She extended her hands for Enoch to sit on one end of the table while Tesha sat on the other end. This was going to be a long day.

TRUTH IS

*T*he day grew into night before this issue was resolved. Chell was patient because she knew that there was more to the story than Tesha was letting on. Through the years, she learned to know when her husband was not being truthful. He had tells, just like in poker. Enoch would start stuttering and sweating profusely whenever he was not being truthful. Tesha, on the other hand, was a whole new ball game. Since they were apart for most of Tesha's young life, Chell was not able to pick up on her tells as easily.

"Look, between you two someone is lying, and I want the truth!" Chell said to no one in particular.

"It ain't me!" screamed Tesha.

Hit dogs will always holla. This gave Chell the opportunity to further interrogate Tesha because there were subtle changes in her demeanor. Instead of being frightened, Tesha took on a defensive stance.

Working in a hospital had shown Chell many victims of sexual abuse and assault. They hardly ever looked their assailant in the face willingly; they wanted to avoid their attackers. Their mannerisms are more timid and uneasy right after their attack. But Tesha was showing all strength and confidence. It was as if she was putting on a show of trying to convince them both that she was right. Enoch, on the other hand, looked exhausted and disappointed. He looked as if he had not slept in days. He had the face of a man on trial for his life.

"Tesha, tell me again what happened."

"Like I said before, Mama, I was down here minding my own business when Enoch called me into your bedroom. When I got in there, he just attacked me. I fought back and ran out of the room."

"That's a li—,"Enoch started.

"Wait, Enoch, let her finish," Chell said cutting him off.

"Tesha, had you been in my room earlier that day."

"No, Mama."

"Then, how did my perfume get on your night gown?"

"Uuhh…He made me put it on. He said that it reminded him of you."

"I thought you said that he just called you up

there and attacked you. When did this conversation take place?" quizzed Chell, knowing now that her daughter was lying.

"He did jump me after he made me put on your perfume." The words came out in a rush. Tesha knew that she was losing her battle.

"How did your panties get in the bed under the covers?"

"I told you, he ripped them off of me. I guess that's where they landed."

"They don't look ripped. Hell, they look brand new."

"They are not new, I been had 'em," Tesha said nervously.

"Then why is the tag still on them?" Chell asked holding the panties in the air.

Enoch's face lit up like a Christmas tree. He knew that Chell had caught Tesha in a lie.

One tiny detail left out. In her haste, Tesha tore off the tags on the side of the panties but forgot about the other one on the inside. She was too through. Her face told it all, and she knew that Chell knew it, too.

"Tesha, how could you?" was all that Chell could muster.

"Cause I hate you, and I don't want to live here! You were never there for me and now that you hide behind church, you think everything is all good. You ain't no better than me, and I'm tired of living in this illusion you call life. As far as I'm concerned, you are still that stank ass crack-head whore who dumped me off on Angie." Tesha stormed off and up the stairs to her room.

The next day, Tesha was on the first thing smoking back to Maplesville. Chell loved her daughter, but she did not know her at all. After all the things Chell had to endure in life from drugs to prostitution, she was not going to let anyone interrupt her new clean life. She worked hard to make a good home in the eyes of God. She and Enoch were doing just fine without anyone else causing trouble. She felt bad for sending Tesha away again, but this was not the child that she had given birth to 16 years ago-- she was a stranger. Plus, Tesha had made it plain and clear that she did not want to be with her. Enough was enough with Tesha. Ever since she came to Bolingbrook, she had been nothing but trouble, and Chell just could not do it anymore. Besides, she will be grown soon.

God, please give me the strength to carry on.
I know that she is my
child, but too much has happened for us
to mend the broken spirits.

LOVÉ

I know that you will take care of her.
Lord, I just pray that you
put it in her heart to forgive me one day.
I am still taking it one
day at a time…I have to stay focused
on my path of recovery.
Father, please step in and take control
because I am lost and
right now I need you to order my steps
in your word. Amen.

DOWN TO SWING

*F*light 756 came in to Birmingham right on time, and Tesha could not wait to get home. She actually missed being in her own bed, and she definitely missed seeing Earl.

This time, I'm not ever leaving. I kind of hate the way things went down with Mama but oh well. Sometimes people get hurt in the game of love. I am going to be 18 soon and then no one will be able to stop me from doing what I want. My mama and her lame ass husband can stay together for all I care; I didn't like him anyway. My trip to Bolingbrook was not all bad because my cousin Tangy showed me a whole new world. We went to the same school, but she taught me how to skip classes without getting caught. We would go downtown to the movies and hang out at her friend Quana's house. We would spend the whole day over there sometimes just hanging out drinking and watching movies.

Quana's house was very nice. Her mother was a shrink and her dad had passed away 2 years ago leaving them a bunch of money. They lived in one of those houses from off television with the huge front and backyard with a pool and guest house. They had an upstairs, downstairs, and a basement. The family room was in the basement. It was complete with a small kitchen, laundry room, bathroom, wet bar, and a full home entertainment center. The main section had a 50 inch flat screen TV with a surround-sound stereo system. This was where we always hung out at after school and on our skip days because her mom was never home.

The most fun I have ever had in my entire life is thanks to Tangy and Quana. One time Tangy and I told our folks that we were going to a slumber party at Quana's house. What we did not share was that Quana's parents were going out of town and that her older sister, Tila, would be watching us. Tila was cool as hell, and she let us have company only if we didn't tell their mom that she was going to be out with her "girlfriend" because she hadn't come out to their family yet. We were all set up in the family room. We had invited Tangy's man and some of his friends over. They brought beer and some weed. I had never really gotten high before. Earl only let me hit it once or twice, but Tangy promised me that it would be fun and that I would like it. She was right. We stayed up all night just smoking and drinking. Malik was Tangy's man, and his friends were Dayon and Kalvin.

The evening was going great. Dayon was with me, Kalvin was with Quana, and of course Malik was with Tangy. After the first six pack of beer was gone, Malik and the guys went to get a 12 pack. It was cool that they were all over 21. Me and the girls just kicked back and smoked some more of the already rolled blunt. On my first pull, I thought I was gonna choke to death. That nasty smoke cut off all my wind and made my throat burn. I knew that Uncle Earl sold weed, but he never really let me smoke it. After a few minutes, I was ready for my second hit.

"It will get easier after a few tries," Tangy said holding in the smoke that she just inhaled.

She and Quana were experts on smoking; I had virgin lungs so they say. When the guys got back, they had bought a bottle of gin instead of the beer that they were supposed to have gotten. They suggested that we play a game of truth or dare. I had heard of this game, but I had never played it, and I wasn't sure if I wanted to. But I was not going to put a damper on things, so I just decided to go with the flow.

We all had to take a shot of gin after each round. The first two rounds were easy with general questions asking if you ever kissed anybody of the opposite sex or same sex; if you ever did it before; or if you ever had a threesome. Everyone was answering their question; then things got a little more exciting. By the time it was my turn again, I was felling real good.

"Tesha, truth or dare?" asked Dayon.

"Fuck it…dare."

"I dare you to kiss Quana on the lips for 5 seconds," he said laughing.

By now we were all nearly naked and tipsy so we didn't have a problem with these sexy requests. So I got up and kneeled down in front of Quana who was sitting between Dayon and Kalvin. We both hesitated for a second; then I grabbed her face and just kissed her square on the mouth.

"Aahh, that ain't no kiss," huffed Malik.

"You said kiss her not tongue her down," I said laughing while I moved back to my seat across from Dayon and Malik.

"Then why don't you show her what a kiss is," slurred Tangy.

I didn't know where she was going with this because Malik was *her* man. Malik slid over to me and planted his juicy lips on mine. He slowly parted my lips with his tongue and let it dance around inside my mouth. I could taste the gin and weed on his tongue. I can't believe that Tangy let him kiss me, but I wasn't gonna stop him. He pulled away from me, I was tingly all over. The same way I felt when Uncle Earl went down on me in the bathroom…I liked it.

Tangy got up and went over to Kalvin and kissed him in the same sexy way that her man had kissed me. Dayon turned to Quana and did the same. The truth and dare game was officially over; this was something totally different. We all took another shot of gin and started a new game. This time we had to undress each other. By now half a gallon of gin was gone, and I was ready for anything. Tangy pulled out some sex cards that she stole from Tila and sat them in the middle of the table. We had to pull a card, read it and do whatever it said.

The first card was Quana's. She read it and put it back on the bottom of the deck. She went over to Kalvin and kissed him on the lips then on his chest. She slid her hands in his boxers and started to massage his dick. He couldn't do nothing but hold his head back. I just sat there in amazement. I had only seen stuff like that on the porno movies that Uncle Earl had showed me during my lessons…it made me hot.

While she jerked him off, Tangy pulled her card. She replaced the card and went over to Quana who was still handling Kalvin. Tangy started rubbing Quana's back and her butt; something told me that this was not her first time touching her. Quana turned slightly so that she was standing in between Tangy and Kalvin. Tangy pulled a chair up so that Quana could put her leg up on it. Tangy got down on her knees in front of Quana and stuck her hand inside of her panties. Quana's mouth fell open as Tangy rubbed her back and forth. I took another shot of gin because I could not believe what I was seeing.

Malik read his card and turned to me. I knew that he always liked me from the way he would look at me when Tangy would leave the room, but I never thought much of it until now. He held his hand out for me to follow him…and I did. He led me over to the sofa. I went to go sit down and he told me to lay back. Malik stood over me for a minute just looking at my body. I must say that I was feeling sexy as hell in my matching wine colored bra and panties. My head was buzzing. Malik was so gentle with me; he must have known that I had not been with a man before even though I had said that I had during the game of truth of dare.

Malik ran his fingers along my waist band and started to pull my panties down. I stopped him. He didn't get mad; he just nodded. He parted my legs with his knee and knelt down between them. I felt his hands rub my body through the sheer material. He bent down and started tongue kissing me on my other set of lips. It felt soooo good. Malik slid my panties to the side and slid his wet tongue inside my honey hole. The strength of his tongue was different from Earl's. Malik's touch was softer. Earl definitely had skills, and with a little practice, Malik would be just as good.

Dayon felt left out, so he went over to Tangy and pulled her away from the tongue lashing she was giving Quana. He told her to sit on the floor and he would be right back. When he returned, he had a small box of Trojans in his hand. He handed one to each of the guys and kept one for himself. Dayon removed the rest of his clothing, which was not much because he was already down to his boxers and t-shirt. This signaled a chain reaction because everyone started taking off their underwear too. I was still a little timid, so my underwear stayed on, but that feeling was slowly fading.

These were some good looking grown men; nothing like the boys I went to school with. Dayon and Malik were the color of milk chocolate. They were about the same height and build. Malik was just a little meatier because he worked out on a regular. Malik had locks in his hair that hung down over his shoulders. He always smelled good and of the three, he was the best dresser. Dayon was sexy as hell. He had dark eyebrows that had a natural arch. He had a small gap between his two front teeth and a dimple in his left cheek. He didn't work out, and it showed, but he was not fat either. Kalvin was kinda skinny with white people's skin, good hair, and green eyes. The ladies loved his dirty drawers. His mother was white but his daddy had to be black because when he took his boxers all the way off, he had one of the biggest dicks I had ever seen. The other two couples wasted no time getting to the sex, but I was a little shy. Malik offered me another drink and I nodded my head yes. When he went to get it, I couldn't help but think about how I wanted my first time to be with Earl. I wondered what he would say if he found out that I had sex with some else.

When Malik returned with my drink, I took it down with one gulp. He sat next to me and started to rub my shoulders. I felt my buzz continue, and I relaxed in Malik's strong hands. He kissed me on my neck, and I just melted. I felt his hands slide down to my titties as he massaged them through the thin fabric. I wanted to be as comfortable as Tangy and Quana who were now getting eaten out and kissing each other. I slid my hand over to Malik's thigh as to give him a signal that I was ready for more. He turned my head to him and kissed me with way more passion than I had ever seen between he and Tangy. I pulled away and stood up in front of him. I slowly removed my bra and then my panties. I could tell instantly that he was pleased. Malik got the condom, opened it and put it on in less than a minute. He then reached for me to sit on his lap facing him, I did. I tried to sit on top of him but it was not working because I was so tight, so he flipped me over and climbed on top. At first there was a lot of pressure and a bit of pain. After he got all the way in and started moving back and forth, it started to feel good. I don't know if it was the alcohol or Malik, but one of them had my head swimming.

Just when I started to get into the rhythm of things, I heard someone say "switch". Then Malik got up and Dayon came over to me and started kissing me. The other girls didn't have a problem with what was happening so I just went with it. Dayon was cute, but he was smaller down there than Malik so I knew that it wouldn't hurt much. As he climbed on top of me I held my breath waiting for him to enter me. I guess he didn't like that position because he stopped and told me to get on my knees facing the wall. I did and he entered me from behind. I felt him then, but I liked Malik better. I just went with the flow and hoped that they called switch soon.

At first was scared of Kalvin. I was thinking that he was just too big and wouldn't fit. But now, I was in the groove and wanted to try his ass anyway. When he came over to me my heart was beating out of my chest. His member was so thick and long...I needed another drink.

"Kalvin, can you get me another drink?" I asked stalling for time.

I looked over to Tangy and all four of them were going at it. Quana was sucking Malik's dick while Tangy was eating her out with Dayon behind Tangy hitting it doggy style. I found out later on that they do this on a regular and had planned to introduce me to the guys one on one so that I could be a part of the festivities. When Kalvin came back, he had a drink for both of us. We both threw the gin back and sat our cups down. I looked back at Quana and decided to try what she was doing. I got down on my knees in front of Kalvin and took him into my mouth. He tasted funny at first, like something sweet and oily but that soon faded away. I didn't know what I was doing, and it was obvious because he stopped me and told me to lie on my back on the floor.

Kalvin slowly climbed between my legs and positioned himself. Kalvin was not fully hard so he rubbed his penis back and forth against my clit, and it felt real good. His dick felt so big against me. I reached for him to kiss me first, and when he did, I guided him into me. He entered with one strong thrust. My breath was caught up in my neck. I opened my mouth, but nothing came out. Kalvin didn't see the expression on my face because he had his head buried in my neck. After a minute I was able to breathe again. His dick was massive. I could not believe how I loosened up to him. He rose up and whispered in my ear, "Damn, you're tight." I started to get comfortable and started to move my hips to his rhythm. Suddenly I felt this rush of pleasure, and it felt like I had to pee. I started breathing faster and faster, Kalvin pumped me faster and deeper. I didn't know exactly what was happening to me, but I didn't want it to stop. From nowhere I started to shake and something exploded in me. I thought I had peed on him. I closed my eyes so tight that all I could see were colorful circles dancing on my eyelids. Kalvin let out a groan and his body started to shake. Then he lay on my chest heaving hard. Our breaths came quickly. I felt beyond drunk.

As I lay there on the floor, the guys got dressed and said their goodbyes. Tangy and Quana just laughed at me.

"I can't move," I whispered.

"That means that it was good," replied Quana as she put on her clothes.

"Kalvin told me to tell you that he liked you," said Tangy over her shoulder.

"I think I pissed on Kalvin."

"Haaa my cuz is a squirter!" laughed Tangy.

"What is a squirter? Is that bad?" I asked.

"Hell naw! Men love that shit. I wish I could do it," said Quana.

From that day on, we would all get together on the weekend. Plus, Kalvin and I started seeing each other one on one. He even taught me how to give head. One time Mama even caught me and Kalvin in my room. He was so scared that he jumped out of the window in nothing but his drawers. I was in trouble for weeks behind that stunt.

"Passengers prepare for landing. The local time is 4:35pm."

The pilot's voice came over the intercom and woke Tesha from her thoughts. She could not wait to see Earl.

I'm Coming Home

"Hello. Who is this?" quizzed Angie.

"It's me, Tesha. Can you come and get me from the airport?"

"The airport? What are you doing back…so soon?"

"Me and Mama had a fight, and here I am."

"Angie, who is that?" asked Earl rolling over to face Angie.

"It's Tesha; she said that she is at the airport."

Earl sat straight up in the bed and looked at Angie with wide eyes. He tried to hide his excitement at having his girl back. He had wanted to ask Angie when she was coming back, but he didn't have the nerve. Plus, he didn't want to raise any suspicions.

"Angie, I'll go get her…you go back to bed," Earl said already getting ready to leave.

"Dang, Earl, I was just getting used to it being just us again," Angie said pouting.

Angie knew that something must have happened up there, and as soon as Earl left, she was going to call Chell to find out. She just knew that Tesha would be staying permanently with her mother. This time, I'm not having any mess out of her. She will stay in a child's place and next year she is getting her ass out of here! I don't give a shit where she goes, but she is getting out of my house forever. And Earl's ass running out of here like she his woman or something, he think he slick. But I'm not having this shit out of him either.

After Angie heard the door slam behind Earl, she reached for her phone. After two rings, Chell answered in a sleepy voice. It was Monday morning, and she and Enoch were still in bed. This was odd.

"Chell, what happened with Tesha?"

"Well good morning to you, too, Angie."

"Bump that, tell me what happened," she ordered.

"It's just was not going to work out that's all," Chell said not really wanting to go into details.

Chell knew that Angie would find some type of pleasure in seeing her fail at being a good mom. Chell knew that Angie was always jealous of her. All through their childhood Angie was hateful to Chell. She would break her toys, cut up her clothes. One time, right before her junior prom, Angie went as far as to cut Chell's hair while she slept.

As adults, things had not changed much, especially after Chell got on drugs. Instead of trying to help and be supportive of her sister, Angie enjoyed the fact that she was down. With Chell clean, it was ten times worse than before. Everyone was so proud of Chell being clean and straightening up her life. In Angie's mind, that is something that Chell should have been doing all along. She doesn't get any praises for staying clean, so what is the big fucking deal?

"Chell, just tell me what happened that you had to send Tesha back."

"To make a long story short, Tesha accused Enoch of trying to rape her. We all discussed the matter, and it turned out that she was lying all along. She also said that she did it because she hated me and didn't want to be here. So I sent her to the only place I knew she would go…back to you."

"DID YOUR HUSBAND TRY TO RAPE MY NIECE?!" Angie yelled.

"No, he did not, and Tesha admitted that she was lying. So if that is all, I have to go." With that, Chell hung up the phone.

I don't need this shit from Angie. Fuck both of them. They must have forgotten that I am from the street, and I have no problem giving them a taste of it. Neither one of them heifers will ruin my marriage, so they can go to hell with all that mess.

As We Lay

"*H*ow was your flight baby girl?" asked Earl with a Kool-aid grin.

"It was fine. Did you miss me?" Tesha asked as she sashayed over to Earl.

"You know I did. What made you want to come back so soon?" he asked unaware of what happened.

Tesha guessed that Earl didn't know what happened, so she decided to give him the condensed version.

"I told mama that Enoch tried to touch me, and she sent me home."

"He did what? Are you alright?" Earl screamed almost hitting the car in front of us.

"Yeah I'm good. He didn't really try anything. I just wanted to come back here to you."

Earl liked that. He knew that Tesha wanted to be with him, and this confirmed his notions. *How can it be wrong if she wants to be with me? I'm not making her do anything she doesn't want to do; hell she'll be 17 next month; that's nearly grown. My mama had me at 15, so as far as I'm concerned Tesha is already a woman,* he thought to himself.

The drive home was peaceful with nonsense chit chat. When Earl took a detour, Tesha didn't know where he was taking her.

"Where are we going?" she quizzed looking out the window.

"Just sit back and ride. I have to make a quick stop."

They pulled up in front of an apartment complex, and Earl told her to come with him. They walked up to the 2nd floor apartment of the building that sat to the right of them. Earl didn't have to knock on the door because he had a key.

"Earl, whose place is this?"

"Mine," he answered smiling and closing the door behind them.

Earl had this place for a few months now. He would bring his other women here so that Angie would not catch him at one of the local motels. He also used this place to do some of his business. The lease was under his deceased brother's name just in case someone started asking questions. It was a shabby one bedroom apartment, but he actually had the place decked out. There was a nice living room sectional on the left wall. He had a big screen TV on the opposite wall next to a 50 gallon aquarium. All the furniture was black with the exception of the cherry wood end tables and coffee table. The room smelled like vanilla, his favorite scent. The kitchen was behind the living room with a small eating area to the side. The bedroom was down the hall on the right.

"Sit down, relax," Earl said motioning for Tesha to sit on the sofa.

"Earl, this is nice. How long have you been hiding this place?"

"Don't you worry about all that…just relax."

Earl went into the kitchen to get them something to drink. He returned with 2 glasses of Paul. He sat down next to her and turned on the television.

"You know that Auntie Angie is gonna be looking for us?"

"I got that covered. If she calls, I'll tell her that I had left my phone in the car."

"What if she asks what took us so long?"

"I'll tell her I got stuck in traffic. Quit worrying, I got this."

Tesha smiled and sat back getting more comfortable. She knew why Earl had brought her here. It had been almost 6 months since the last time they were alone. She didn't even get to say bye because Angie got her up early on a Sunday morning and sent her off. Earl didn't even know she was gone because he thought Angie was getting ready for church when she got up singing. He found out later when she came home that she had dropped her off at the airport. They had it out that night. Tesha called Earl almost every day from the cell phone that he had secretly bought her, but after her escapades with Tangy, those calls were few and far in between. He could hardly get her on the line. Her excuse was always the same, her mom had her doing something and she couldn't talk. He knew those were lies, but what could he really say?

Earl went into the bedroom and came out with a DVD. He was more than ready to touch Tesha, but he didn't want her to know how much he missed her. He slid the disk in and hit play. Out of nowhere, naked ass and moans of pleasure filled the tiny room. He scrambled to turn the volume down all the while Tesha was laughing at his look of shock.

"I should have known better, those things just pop on don't they? No credits or nothing; just bam! Ass and tits."

Earl regained his composure and slid next to Tesha on the sofa. While he was in the room, he had popped half of a Viagra, so now he was stalling for time so that the pill could take full effect. He didn't really need it but he wanted to make a lasting first impression. He asked her some more questions about her trip and tried to act like he really cared. Every other question was about her mother, but Tesha didn't catch on because she didn't know of their past dealings. Earl did like Tesha, but he was more concerned with Chell. He knew that he could never have Chell again, and Tesha was the next best thing, so he was satisfied with the consolation prize and planned to take full advantage of the situation.

"Tesha, I really missed you baby."

"Why? Angie was here."

"Fuck Angie. You know she can't do me like you can. Her ass done got too damn big. I don't even like being with her like that no more."

Tesha liked when Earl put Angie down. It made her feel special, like she was better than her aunt. Truth is, Earl was lying. Angie was some of the best ass he ever had, next to Chell that is.

"Yeah, whatever…you still sleep with her."

"Sometimes I have to; that don't mean I like it. You're the one I want to be with," he said rubbing her shoulder.

Earl pulled Tesha to him and started kissing

her. He really did miss her kisses. Tesha had very full lips, just like he liked them. The fuller the lip, the better the head was the way he looked at it.

"Baby, do you want to try something new?" he asked through kisses.

"Yeah, what?"

"Let's do what they are doing on the movie."

Earl turned Tesha's head towards the screen as he started to kiss her neck and shoulder. The couple on the screen was in the 69 position. Tesha had never seen that position before, but she found it a perfect way to show off her new skills as well as get pleased. They undressed and went into the bedroom. This would be the first time that they would go all the way. All the other times was just kissing, touching, some hand jobs, and him orally pleasing her. Tesha was more than ready to go all the way, but she knew she had to act like it was her first time.

Earl lay on his back on the bed and Tesha climbed on top of him facing his feet. In no time they had taken each other in their mouths. Many nights went by where Earl longed for the taste of Tesha's sweet black pussy. He knew that today was the day for them to finally go all the way. He thought to himself that she was surprisingly pretty good at giving head. Her teeth didn't scrape him or nothing. Earl could hardly concentrate on what he was supposed to be doing. Tesha had his head going. She was sucking his dick like it was a popsicle, and she didn't want to waste a drop. He had to give it to her, she was better than Angie ever was.

Tesha knew that her practice with Kalvin was paying off buy the way Earl was moaning. She noticed that he was slacking up on his job on her so she slowed down. She felt his tongue rub against her clit with such force that she stopped in mid suck to savor the moment. Earl grabbed her hips and pulled her closer to him and held on so that she could not move. His mouth worked overtime on her. He was always good at eating her pussy. No one had ever come close to his skills in that area. This became their favorite position.

"Turn over baby," he whispered.

Earl got ready to position himself between her legs, but Tesha stopped him and pushed him back on the bed. This was new for him because he was always the dominate one. He wondered if she had been fucking someone else while she was in Bolingbrook. He knew better than to say something for fear of ruining the mood; he still was hard, and she needed to take care of it. Tesha climbed on top of Earl and in one quick motion she had him inside her. She started off slow then sped up after he was comfortably inside her walls. Earl was in heaven. It had been too long since he was rode like this; he and Angie only did it doggy style because of her size. Tesha had learned quite a few things from Kalvin during her short stay. She knew how to control her vaginal muscles by squeezing and releasing them several times a day. She used this technique when riding a man. Kalvin showed her how to squeeze them tight coming up and release her grip going down. He showed her how to just ride the head then swallow him whole and repeat the process. This drove Earl wild.

"Where did you learn that?" he could not help asking realizing that he had a new favorite position.

"From watching movies," she lied knowing he could never know the truth.

Earl flipped her over and entered her from the back thinking that he would have the upper hand…wrong. Kalvin was a good teacher and she knew how to throw it back with the best of em. Every new position Earl tried to put her in was another one where she took charge. Tesha was a good student, and Kalvin taught her well. Earl was much smaller than Kalvin was so it was easier for her to control him. Earl didn't know what hit him, but he was hooked. Since that day, he couldn't wait to get her alone. His secret place became their secret place where Tesha was the lady of the house.

After Tesha had milked Earl for all that he was worth, money included, they got cleaned up and headed home to Angie whom they knew was surly sitting in the window waiting on them.

HOME

"What took yawl so long to get back?" questioned Angie.

"The traffic was bad; then we went to get something to eat. Here we brought you something to eat." Tesha jumped in with more confidence than she had ever shown towards Angie.

Angie didn't buy that excuse, but there was no evidence to prove otherwise. She saw that there was something different about Tesha. She held her head up more and looked her directly in the eye when she talked to her. Before, Tesha was very timid and damn near afraid of her own shadow, but now it is like she had aged 10 years. Not much had changed around there. Angie was still big as all get out with the same nasty attitude. They had made some changes to their home though. There was a new living room set as well as wood-looking laminate tiles on the floor. It gave the living room a more polished look.

"Tesha, next week we are going to get you back into high school."

"Yeah, I was thinking about that. I don't want to go back to school. Can't I just get my GED instead? I got the grades, Auntie, and I know that I can pass the test."

Angie thought on this for a minute and asked Tesha why she didn't want to go back to school.

"It's not that I don't want to go back. It's just that since it is in the middle of the year, they are gonna try and put me back a grade."

Angie knew that this was true. When her and Chell would go back and forth from Maplesville to Bolingbrook as kids they always got set back a grade

"Well if you ain't gonna go to school you are gonna have to get a job."

"Okay, Auntie, I'll start looking tomorrow." Tesha was so excited because now she didn't have to ever leave the house. Earl had already run the plan past her on the way home. He had started his own landscaping company and told Tesha if she convinced Angie to let her get her GED, she could come work for him and get paid under the table so they can't take the taxes out.

Later that night Earl talked to Angie about letting Tesha work for him, and she did not like it one bit.

"Why can't she find her own job, Earl?"

"Why should she? They ain't gonna pay her as much as I will, and you know it. She ain't gonna make shit without her diploma. You know I'ma take care of her. Plus, I want to keep the business in the family…ain't no need to be giving money to no stranger."

"But I want her to be around people her own age and make some friends," Angie said trying to sound sad for Tesha's sake.

"This ain't about friends, Angie. This is about her making her own money. Then you ain't got to give her none." He knew that might do the trick because Angie was stingy with her cash.

"Plus, I want someone who I can trust with our money. You know Tesha has always been good with money."

"I know but –"

"Angie, what is the problem?" Earl asked a little upset by her not agreeing with him.

"Nothing, Earl, do what you want." Angie didn't want to fight, so she just let it go.

The months leading up to the summer seemed to fly by. Where has the time gone? Things have been ok since Tesha came back, but I still need some answers.

Let me call Mags again. I have been calling my mother for weeks trying to find out what really happened up there to make Chell send Tesha home. Whenever I bring up Tesha or Enoch, she all of a sudden has to go to the bathroom or something and hurries off the phone. Chell stopped answering my calls long ago, and Mags is acting like I'm bothering her or something. Tesha is my only niece, and I want to know what is going on. I guess I will just have to leave her another message:

"Mama, call me as soon as you get this message. I love you bye."

ADORE

*T*esha just adored Earl. He was always there for her. Whenever Aunt Angie got on her for something, Earl always stepped in to stop her. There was nothing Earl would not do for Tesha. If Angie would not give it to her or buy it for her, she knew Earl would. Angie and Earl have bumped heads many a day about Tesha. One day after Angie yelled at Tesha and sent her to bed, she overheard them talking about her.

"Earl, you let her get away with too much," Angie said while folding the laundry.

"So what, she a kid, they supposed to do stuff."

"Yeah they supposed to mind also, but she do as she pleases with you backing her up."

"It will be ok Angie, you fuss too much."

"I'm gonna start beating her ass if she don't start doing as I say."

"And if you do I'm gonna start beating yo ass.

Don't you dare lay a hand on her."

Earl's tone was controlled but full of power. Angie knew from experience that he was not playing. Earl didn't mind Angie talking shit all the time because he knew how to shut her ass up. Sometimes it called for a harsh tone, and sometimes it called for a slap in the face. Either way, she'd shut the fuck up. Angie had noticed that more often those actions were because of Tesha.

Tesha noticed it, too. She knew that Uncle Earl favored her over Angie because of the way he looked at her and talked about Angie when she was not around. He always talked about how cute Tesha was getting and how fat Angie was getting. About how Tesha was growing up to be a nice young lady and how the older Angie got, the meaner she got. Earl always compared the two of them. After a while, Tesha began to believe him and got the big head. Never once did she ever see this as a set up. Earl had big plans for Tesha.

FAMILY REUNION

*T*he end of the summer was finally here. This year the family had planned to go to Florida for their reunion. They were planning a day at Disney World, and the rest of the weekend would be spent at the hotel around the pool and sight-seeing. Things with Angie and Earl had only gotten worse since Tesha's return. They hardly ever had any alone time because he was always working which meant that he and Tesha were spending more time together. If it wasn't work, they were fishing or hunting. Earl used to try to get Angie to go on his sporting events even though he knew she would decline. After so many no's, he just stopped asking. With Tesha, things were different. She liked to do those things. He had even bought her a gun and her own fishing pole so that they could go at any time without having to borrow someone else's.

Angie occupied her time with shopping and

her new job. She worked at the local casino 10 hours a day. After a while, she stopped worrying about them two because in her mind, she already had Earl and had nothing to worry about. Earl had been with Angie for damn near 20 years now, and if he was gonna leave her, he would have already. Every now and then there would be some talk about Earl and Tesha, but to Angie that was just some miserable people trying to stir up some mess in her home.

"Yawl better be ready to roll out in the next 10 minutes or you two will be walking to Florida!" Angie yelled to Earl and Tesha as she was walking out to the car.

Earl and Tesha were too busy trying to steal one last kiss because they knew that in Florida they would have to be cool because all eyes would be on them. They also knew that they needed to hurry the hell up cause Angie didn't give idle threats… she would really leave their asses.

All three of them took turns driving the 6 hours to their destination. Earl had taught Tesha to drive years ago, but she still didn't have her license. From the outside looking in, they were a typical family on a typical vacation. There were no arguments, and everyone had a good time. The hotel was only a few minutes from Disney World, and the room had a fantastic view. The suite had a master bedroom, living room with a pull out couch, and a kitchenette. Once they got there, they got checked into their room and headed out to greet the rest of the family.

Almost all of the Anderson family had arrived. The family was spread out all over the U.S. There were car tags from Illinois, New York, Alabama, Georgia, Connecticut, Michigan, New Jersey, and Mississippi. Since the early 1980's, the Andersons have had a reunion every year. The last reunion was on a cruise to the Grand Cayman Islands in Mexico. Most of the reunions are held in Maplesville because that is where the family originated.

Tesha thought that it was really good to see some of her cousins again, but she didn't want to hear any mess from the older members of her family. Too many times her great uncles and aunts have told her to watch her mouth and stay in a child's place. Tesha always felt that the women were jealous and the men must want her. This year was different though. Tesha's cousins didn't have too much to say to her. Majority of the girls were all older than her and saw her as a troublesome child. They used to try to talk some sense into her, but her attitude just pushed them away. The other cousins her age and younger were still talking about boys while

Tesha's mind was on grown men. The boys in the family didn't pay her any mind either because they were too busy looking at the females by the pool.

"Tesha, do you want to come with us to the amusement park?" asked Tesha's cousin Sasha.

"Who all is going?" Tesha asked holding her hand up shielding her eyes from the sun.

"Uncle James is going to drop all of us off," Sasha said with a wave of her hand towards the other teenagers.

"Nah, I'm kinda tired from the drive down here, so I might go lay down so I can be ready for tonight," Tesha said in the much too grown attitude that she had developed over the past few years.

"What chu mean you're tired from the drive?" quizzed Sasha.

"Well, unlike you my dear, I had to drive down here. That's what I mean. So, no thank you." With that said Tesha rolled her eyes and turned and walked away.

Tesha talked like she was 27 instead of 17. Her tone was so full of attitude that no one really liked to talk to her. Her attitude towards life was "been there, done that" while everyone else her age was still trying to find their way. The way Angie talked to others had rubbed off on her, and she had no respect for anyone one but Earl. Anyone who said anything to her received attitude. So most family members just ignored her because they knew she didn't know any better. Plus, if you did say something to her, Angie would try to go off. She didn't like the girl, but she wouldn't let anyone else say nothing to her.

Most of the family knew that something was going on between Earl and Tesha. Their behavior was consistent with a male/female relationship, not an uncle/niece type a thing. Many family members tried to tell Angie to open up her eyes and see what was going on right under her nose, and she didn't want to hear it. Angie had said more than once that no one was so concerned when it was happening to them so why now? To most this was the stupidest thing they had ever heard, especially since they didn't know what she was talking about.

Night time fell as the last of the Anderson family arrived. The kids were put to bed by 10pm, and the adults were hanging around the heated pool.

"Tesha, where do you think you are going?" asked Angie.

"I'm going with yawl to sit around the pool," Tesha said gathering a beach towel headed for the door.

"Ummm no ma'am. Only adults are going to the pool, and the last time I checked you were still a child. This room is where you will be 'til morning."

"But auntie I want to go to the pool with yawl!" Tesha whined.

"I…said…no! Don't make me tell you again," Angie said with her hands on her hips as a dare for Tesha to try her.

"Yes ma'am." Tesha wasn't that foolish. She knew when to back down from her aunt.

"Come on, Earl."

Tesha was left in the room alone with the remote. She couldn't believe that Earl left her there so he could be with Angie. *I'll fix his black ass. He thinks he gonna fuck me whenever he wants to then push me to the side to be with her, shittin' me. I ain't having that mess,* she thought.

Tesha checked to see if the coast was clear before she opened the sliding window of their suite. She pulled out a pack of Salem cigarettes, a habit that she had picked up from hanging with Earl. They would smoke after sex, but his Newports were too strong for her, so she found her own brand. Angie knew that she smoked, but she knew she couldn't stop her either. And as long as she bought her own smokes, Angie really didn't care. Angie didn't care what Tesha did but she was more than ready to bite the head off anybody else who said something about her.

A knock at the door brought Tesha in from her smoke break.

"Who is it?"

"It's me, open the door."

She knew the voice, so she opened the door just wide enough for him to come in.

"What do you want?" Tesha asked walking back over to the window.

"You," said Earl.

"Then you shouldn't have left me alone."

"You know I had to, but I'm back now," he said tying to sound convincing.

"Well, what can I do for you?" she inquired trying not to sound pleased that he had come back to her.

"Come here and let me show you."

Tesha closed the window and pulled the curtain shut. She ran over to Earl and jumped into his arms. They kissed until they were both very excited.

"We have to hurry," he whispered.

Tesha had already changed into her night dress for bed. Earl turned her around to the table that was in the sitting area of the room and lifted her dress. He was in her within seconds. She was so warm around him, and he knew that he would not be able to last for much longer. Tesha held on to the chair for balance and arched her back so that Earl could go deeper. He was getting it good when they heard loud laughter coming from the hallway. Earl pulled out and ran to the bathroom while Tesha straightened her gown and lay on the bed pretending to watch television. When Angie entered the room, Earl flushed the toilet on cue. Angie looked at Tesha for answers as to who was in their room, but before she could answer Earl walked out adjusting his clothes.

"I thought you were going to the store?" Angie asked as she closed the door.

"I left my wallet and needed to pee," he lied.

Without even looking in her face, he left the room without another word.

The rest of the trip went as planned. Earl and Tesha opted not to chance it again because the last time was a little too close for comfort. Angie was surprisingly pleasant for the rest of the trip. She was always a ball of laughs as long as she had an audience. The family all enjoyed each other and vowed to make the Disney trip an option for future family reunions.

On the last day Earl had a nasty fall by the pool. There was a big thud and Earl was flat on his back.

He couldn't say for sure what happened. Everyone kept asking him how he fell and the answer remained the same "I don't know". No one actually saw him fall because they were all having fun in the pool. They heard him hit the ground though. The truth is that Angie had caught him looking at Tesha a little too long and she tripped his ass up while he was walking backwards past her. He really didn't know how he fell because he was too busy looking at Tesha in her 2-piece bikini. Angie swore that he must have tripped on a discarded shoe or something...she was partially right.

For the next few days after the trip to Florida, Earl was in severe pain. But like a man, he refused to go to the doctor. Instead he decided to doctor on himself with some home remedies. Angie had told him to make an appointment as soon as they got home because he said that he had hurt his back when he fell. After a few weeks of rubbing liniment on his back and treating the pain with liquor he was forced to the ER. In the end Earl needed to have surgery to correct a slipped disk.

I'm Going Down

"Girl, Earl gonna kill me,"

She knew how Earl felt about his truck. Earl had just bought a used Ford Explorer. He spent all his money and Angie's on fixing it up. By the time he was done with everything the truck looked brand new. He gave it a fresh jet black paint job, new interior carpet, and put that bad boy on some 22 inch rims. He loved that truck more than he cared for her. And Angie knew that when she finally got home there would be a fight over her letting it run out of gas on I-85.

"You didn't do it on purpose, calm down, he'll understand," Nay said trying to be reassuring.

"Oh no he aint," I said. I know that nut is going to act a fool when he find out about this shit. I don't understand how a man can care more about a truck than his own wife. I'm just gonna keep quiet and see how this plays out."

Nay and Angie had to walk about half a mile in what felt like the coldest day of the winter to the gas station and phone Earl. No one stopped to help them. In this day and time this is a plus and a minus because people are crazy. You think someone is a Good Samaritan and they turn out to be a psychopath. Once they arrived at the gas station it felt like reaching the promise land. The warmth was welcomed with both hands. Nay went to buy some coffee while Angie made the call to Earl.

"Earl, can you come get us from the Quick Serve?" Angie asked in an unsteady voice, scared of what he might say.

"What? Angie, where's my truck?" Earl was hot already.

"It's on the side of the highway. I ran out of gas."

"How the fuck did you run out of gas? I bet you was running your fat mouth with Nay and not paying attention to my shit. Buy some gas and take it back to the truck."

"I ain't got no money left," Angie said barely above a whisper.

"See, this the shit I be talking 'bout. Get yo ass back to my truck before somebody steals it."

"You expect me to walk back to the truck and wait for you when you can come get me from the store and buy the gas?" she quizzed.

"Oh, now you want to think. You better be at my truck or I know somethin'." The line went dead.

Angie had to save face and get herself together in front of Nay. So she said that she was going to use the ladies' room. I have got to get myself together. Hell, Nay life ain't perfect either, but she don't need to know everything about mine. I know this nigga gonna act a fool with me when we get to the truck. I just pray that he takes it easy in front of Nay. Ever since he got that damn truck he has been trippin'. Hell, I helped his no count ass get the damn thing in the first place. Who bought those 22 inch rims? I did! Who gave up some of the down payment? I did! I'm getting pissed just thinking about it. I got a trick for that ass. He must have forgotten that I'm better at cutting the fool then he is, and all I need is a reason...but this ain't one of 'em.

"Nay will you believe that Earl wants us to walk back to the truck and wait for him there?" I said shaking my head.

"Why?" Nay quizzed

"Girl you know that nigga is throwed off", I joked.

"Angie you know you my girl and all but it is cold as hell out there."

"Fine! You aint gotta come. I'll go back by my damn self. Some friend you are."

With that said Angie was out of the door. Nay knew that she had better join her or their friendship would never be the same. Besides Angie was her best girlfriend and she knew that if the shoe was on the other foot Angie would be there for her.

Earl had his brother Keith take him down to get his truck. Earl put a gallon of gas into the tank and cranked it up all the while giving Angie the stank eye. She shrugged it off still trying to save face. She tried to act like she was mad with him so that he wouldn't say anything to her that would set her off. It was working until it was time to load up. Nay hopped in the truck with Keith and drove off. Earl turned to Angie and just shook his head while getting behind the wheel of his truck. When Angie went to get into the truck, Earl locked the door. Angie yanked on the door and yelled to Earl, "Stop playing, it's cold out here, open the damn door!" "You shoulda thought about that shit before; get back the best way you know how." Then he just drove off.

Nay was looking in the rear view mirror and saw how Earl had left Angie on the side of the road, she urged Keith to go back for her friend. Angie had been walking for about 20 minutes when Keith came back to pick her up. She knew he did this behind his brother's back because Earl would be pissed even more if he knew that Keith came for her. Keith always liked Nay, so she knew that if it weren't for her she would have had to walk all the way home which was more than 3 miles. She was so embarrassed.

"Thanks Keith."

"No problem. You know how my brother can get over that truck. Give him a few hours to calm down, and he'll be alright."

I remained silent the rest of the ride to Nay's house. I think I will lay low at Nay's until he cools off. The only thing I hate is that Nay has four bad ass kids who seem to be always on a sugar high.

After a few hours, I had Nay carry me on home. I knew that I would have to face Earl sooner or later, so I may as well get it over with. It had to be about 11 p.m. when I got home. The house was quiet and the coast looked clear. Or so I thought.

"Where you been Angie?" The voice came out of the shadows.

"At Nay's" I said trying to sound irritated so that he would back off.

"Oh, I see. You musta been with your other nigga, huh?"

"Did I say that?"

"You don't have to because I already know," Earl said moving into the light so that Angie could see him.

"And how you gonna tell me where I been? If you cared, you wouldn't have left me on the side of the road," I said moving towards the bedroom. I tried to undress quickly so that I could hop into bed and pretend to be sleep.

"I know because I called Nay's, and she said that you weren't there. So again, where you been?"

What the hell is he talking about? I thought to myself. *I know that I had been with Nay since earlier today, so why would she tell him that I wasn't there? That must have been the phone call she got when I was in the bathroom. I see this is going to be a long night.*

"Earl, she must have said that because she knew that I didn't want to talk to you," I said with my back to him.

"Nah, I know you weren't there. You must think I'm some kinda fool. Yo lying ass was out whoring around," he said raising his voice.

"Earl, you talking crazy. You been drinking?"

"So what? That ain't got nothing to do with you tricking."

"For the last time, I ain't been out tricking. And would you lower your voice before you wake the dead?"

"You right. Come outside and talk to me."

"I don't want to go outside; it's late and it's cold."

"I don't give a shit. Get your fat ass up and come outside."

I swear this nigga is sick. The temperature had dropped to about 40 degrees outside. We usually go outside to argue so that Tesha would not hear us but this is ridiculous. I knew that he didn't want to wake her up, but I still didn't want to go outside. Reluctantly, I got up and went outside to see what the hell he wanted. I wrapped my house coat around me and slid into my slippers and followed Earl outside. I knew this was a bad idea, but he was not going to let up until he had his say.

"Angie, why do you always have to act like you ain't got no damn sense? If something had happened to my truck what were you gonna do then, huh?"

"I don't –" was all I got out before a sharp pain took over my face. I was stunned and frozen in place. I tried to back away from Earl, but he caught me by my arm and yanked me back to him.

"Let go, you're hurting my arm," I said through clinched teeth.

Earl proceeded to slap me, shake me and curse me out for leaving his truck. I couldn't believe that he was really this mad at me. Through tears I pleaded with him to stop hitting me. I tried to fight him back, but my hits didn't faze him.

"You think I don't know who you were with bitch?" Earl gritted though his teeth.

"Earl, I swear that I wasn't with nobody."

I tried to protect my face so that I would not have any bruising. After that last time he actually blacked my eye, I learned to just take the body shots because they are easier to hide.

"Why you keep lying? Just tell the truth," he said pushing me away from him. As I stumbled back, I fell over a rock and landed flat on my ass.

"I ain't lying. You just don't want to believe me."

I don't know where I got the nerve, but I got up and jumped in his face.

"I ain't gonna say it no more. I was with Nay! Where the fuck you been while you questioning me? I'm so sick of you accusing me of shit. If I wanted somebody else I woulda been left. You know what, that is exactly what I should do…leave your monkey ass. I'm tired of this back and forth shit with you, Earl."

It felt good to say that. I felt stronger, and I could see that Earl was taking my words in. I felt confident and turned to walk back into the house. Then all of a sudden I felt a burst of pain on my arm then another. I fell onto the steps and rolled over to see Earl swinging an iron pipe at me. I rolled off the steps onto the grass. He missed striking me by an inch. I got up and ran over to his truck. I knew he wouldn't risk hitting his precious truck, and I was right. Through labored breath, I yelled for him to stop. When my neighbor's light came on, he dropped the pipe and lowered his voice. I ran over to my neighbor's house and banged on the front door. Mr. Mills was my closest neighbor. He was an elderly gentleman who had lived in the same house for over fifty years, and I knew that he had heard all the commotion going on outside.

"Mr. Mills, it's me Angie please open the door." I was sobbing heavily by now and prayed that Mr. Mills would hurry.

"Who is it?" A strong unfamiliar voice came from the other side of the door.

"It's me, Angie, your neighbor, please open up," I cried.

The door swung open with such a force that I knew it was not Mr. Mills; it was his son Damian. He had a shot gun in his right hand and was grabbing me into the house with his left.

"Are you okay?" he asked looking at my bloody lip and torn night clothes.

"No, can I please use your phone to call my cousin to come get me?"

"Yeah, sure, you want me to call the police?"

"No! I'll be fine. My cousin will come get me. She stays around the corner."

The last thing I needed was to get the police involved with all the dope Earl had stashed around the house. They were just looking for a reason to come up in there and bust him. I hated Earl right now, but if I got the law involved, he would make my life a living hell. I called my cousin Ella; she lived about five minutes from here. I looked at the clock by the phone and it was 2 am. I knew she would probably be asleep, but I didn't have anyone else to call. After about five rings, an anxious voice answered.

"Hello."

"Ella, you up?"

"Yeah, who is this?"

"It's Angie, can you come get me?"

"Where are you?"

"At Mr. Mills, Earl jumped on me."

"Ok, I'm on my way."

The line went dead. I really hated to wake her at this time of night. She is seven months pregnant with her first child, and I know she needs her rest. I knew she would come for me though. We grew up together in Bolingbrook. She looked up to me because she was an only child. When she was little, she used to follow me around all the time. I am older than her, so I was like her big sister. She can't stand Earl, but she usually minds her own business, so I know that this will stay between us.

AFTER THE PAIN

*A*ngie didn't sleep well that night at Ella's. She was bothered by thoughts of her past that just would not let her rest. After tossing and turning for over an hour, Angie decided to get up and go to the kitchen for a cup of hot tea. Ella's kitchen had a patio that overlooked her spacious backyard full of mature trees; it was a beautiful view of nature. Angie opened the curtains at the patio door and looked outside. It had started to rain. There was an amber glow coming from the security light which reminded Angie of a morning sunrise. Unlike Angie's normal view from her home that overlooked Mitchell's, Ella's place was very peaceful day or night. After what Angie had gone through with Earl, this was a much needed change of scenery. As she took a seat at the kitchen table to have her tea, Angie immediately got lost in her mind and was haunted with the memories of her past.

The sun was high and bright burning the memories deep into my soul. My legs were starting to cramp from being in the same twisted position for such a long time. I had to get up, but my whole body ached. I could tell that my face had swollen up because of the tightness around my eyes and mouth. My eyes burned from wasted tears. I tried to clear my throat and spit, but it was dry and scratchy from my unheard cries. I sat up and tried to straighten my legs. They were dirty with grass and dry blood…my blood. My insides hurt with every movement. The spot between my legs that my mama always said to keep to myself was exposed for the whole world to see; they had ripped my dress. I gathered the shreds of cloth and tried to cover myself as I walked to the creek. Every step hurt so badly, it felt like I had been cut open with a knife. The creek water was so cool on my burning limbs; I didn't care that I could not swim because if I drowned like lil Millie, I would probably be better off. I waded through the water washing my body of their filth. I splashed water in my mouth to clean it of its foul taste. My tears began to fall again as the creek's water soothed the stinging between my legs. I perched myself up on a submerged rock. The water came up to my waist and covered me in its waves. I just sat there with my face in my hands weeping.

"Angie…Angie…you out here gal?"

It was Chell, but I didn't answer.

"Angie, stop hiding, Granny's been looking for you."

"Chell…Chell," I called to her.

"Angie, what cha sitting in the middle of the creek for? Come from out there 'fo you kill yaself."

"Chell, help me off this rock."

"You got out there, so you can get back," she said folding her arms across her chest.

"I can't. I'm hurt,"

Chell hurried into the water to me with wide eyes.

"What's wrong, Angie? What happened to your face, gal?"

I looked up to my sister with dry tears on my face and a hollow heart.

"You should have been here with me," I said with a scowl.

"What?"

"They wouldna hurt me if you were here!" I screamed.

"What? Who hurt you?" Chell searched her little sister's face for answers but found none.

"Why didn't you come with me like I asked? Mama said for you to watch after me, but you didn't. It's your fault that those boys hurt me. I hate you!"

I got off the rock and waded to the shore. I walked home with Chell following behind me asking me what happened. I never turned to her. That was the last time I ever looked up to my big sister.

Chell and I didn't speak for the next few days. As a matter of fact, I didn't say much to anyone and no one even noticed. Just like I thought, they didn't love me. When anyone would ask me what happened to my face, I lied and told them that I fell. I was too ashamed to admit what had happened. I had a constant pain in my stomach and all I could do for some type of relief was to hold it and rock.

It was finally Friday, the first day of our family reunion. On Sunday we were heading back home and saying goodbye to Granny's house. Folks from all over started pouring in. They all seemed so happy to see each other, it was sickening. They all spoke to me, but most of their comments they could have kept to themselves. They always said something like "Ooh Angie, you're getting so big" or "Angie, I hardly recognized you 'cause you done got so fat," but the topper was always "Angie, why can't you be more like Chell?" I hated being compared to Chell.

Here comes my Mama making her way through the crowd towards me. I wanted to tell her what happened but she never asked me how I got those bruises.

"Angie baby, what you doing sitting over here all by yourself just rocking like a crazy person?"

"Just sitting here Mama."

"Well, I'm tired of you just sitting there. Come with me. I want you to meet some of ya folks."

Mama grabbed me by the hand, and I met second, third, and fourth cousins. I met uncles and aunties that I never knew existed all with smiles and hugs. There were even some people there who looked like they were white. I didn't want anyone to touch me, but for my Mama's sake, I smiled and hugged everyone I met. I stopped giving in when I met Uncle Raymond. My mama told me that this was her younger half brother. He was high yella with a full face of hair. Raymond reached for me and caused me to jump back onto my Mama's foot. It was the same face that I had seen in the woods. This was turning out to be a real family reunion.

I knew I saw something in his eyes-- my Mama. They had the same eyes-- light brown -- and when they caught the sun at the right angle, they changed colors. They must have gotten them from their daddy. I never knew Bill Thomas other than in photos because he never came around. The story was that he was half Indian and half white. And from eavesdropping on my Mama's sisters, he was the reason Grandpa used to fight Grandma all the time. From the looks of my Granny's kids, the first three were his because they all had what we used to call good hair and pretty eyes. The other four were dark like me with nappy hair. My aunts were always jealous of mama because she was so pretty; Chell took after Mama.

"Angie, get off my foot! Where are your manners? Give your Uncle Raymond a hug, gal." Mama pushed me into the arms of my attacker.

"I don't wanna, Mama," I said trying to back away from Raymond.

"Gal, stop being foolish," she said with a final shove to my back.

I landed against Raymond's chest and he wrapped his arms around me and squeezed me tight with a laugh. I felt like a ton of bricks had landed on my head. My feet felt like lead was in them. I couldn't breathe. Everything was spinning like that time I got into Grandpa's moonshine. I started panting…everything went black.

You know that thin space of time between sleep and being awake where mind can wake up before your body? I love that place…it feels good. I can hear my Mama calling my name, but I can't bring my body to move. I don't want to leave this peaceful place in my mind, nothing can harm me here. I wonder if this is what death is like.

"Angie baby, please wake up," my Mama cried.

Something cold hit my face, and I gasped for air. It was my grandma splashing cold water on me.

"I'm sorry Mama." I started to cry and threw my arms around her neck. I held her as tight as I could until she pried herself free. I looked around and everyone was stuffed in the tiny room off the kitchen. I was surprised to see the look of worry on some of their faces, but when they saw that I was alright, most of them left and went back outside. There were only four people left with me-- Mama, Chell, Granny, and Aunt Betty.

"Angie, what's wrong with you?"

"Mama, he attacked me!" I screamed.

"What? Who attacked you?"

"Raymond and his friends attacked me in the woods."

"What? Girl, you just met him today. What are you talking about?"

"I know Mama, but it was him. I seen his face."

"Child, this heat got you talking crazy. That boy ain't never seen you before today. How can you say sucha thing?"

"But Mama—"

"I don't want to hear it, Angie. Why you always gotta try and get some attention, huh? Saying something like this can really hurt somebody; this ain't something you joke about," Mama said rising to stand up over me.

"Mama, I ain't joking. Ask Chell."

"Chell, what is this girl talking about?" Mama asked turning to my sister who was standing by the door.

"I don't know, Mama. I found her sitting in the creek with a beat up face…I thought she got into another fight. She didn't tell me Raymond did anything to her," Chell said with wild eyes.

"Then it's settled. Angie, you fell pretty hard out there. Raymond was the last person you saw and you just dreamed that he was attacking you. Sometimes the heat can play tricks on your mind and make you see stuff that really ain't there, understand?"

"But Mama—" I said trying to get out of bed.

"No 'but Mama' I don't want to hear another word about this foolishness. You lay in here and cool down. I'll bring you somethin' to eat later… just rest."

And just like that, they were gone, and I was alone again. Mama believed Chell over me -- again. Outside my door, I could hear Aunt Betty and Mama talking.

"You know Mag's I did hear that that boy likes to mess with lil kids."

"Are you sure? Do you think Angie is telling

the truth?

"I don't know."

"Betty, you tryna tell me that my baby was messed with by my own brother? I'll kill 'em!"

"Hold on, Maggie. Look, I love Angie just as much as you do, but what's done is done and nothing is gonna change that. Look, that family is claiming us now that Bill's wife is dead. You know them the richest folks around, and when daddy dies, we will be entitled to some of that money. I'm tired of living like this. That man got one foot in the grave, and it's just a matter of time before we cash in. Don't mess this up over something you can't prove or change. Besides, what man in his right mind would touch Angie? Chell maybe but Angie, child please!"

With every word, my stomach turned in knots. I could not believe what my auntie was saying. It was like I didn't matter at all. As I fought back tears, I could feel my heart breaking some more. Then and there in my Granny's back room, I made a vow to myself to look out for only me. I had to make my own way by any means, and anybody who got in my way had to fall. If my own Mama and sister won't stand up for me, nobody else will. God made me big for a reason, and now it's time to use what he gave me. From this point on, nobody else will ever hurt me again.

Lean on Me

"What are you doing up?"

The voice came from behind Angie; it was Ella.

"Oh nothing, just thinking. Did I wake you?"

"Child please, this is our normal snack time," joked Ella as she rubbed her protruding belly.

The two laughed at Ella's comment which really lightened Angie's heart. Ella knew that things in Angie's world were not great and considering what she went through this morning, there was no need to open that door at this moment. Instead, she just fixed them a snack, and for the next hour or so, the cousins just talked about the good 'ol days until they were sleepy again.

Later that day, Angie was awakened by the smell of something wonderful. Ella had gotten up a few hours earlier and decided to fix Angie something to eat. Ella enjoyed having folks over to try some of her creations. Today she made a simple chicken and waffle meal with fresh orange juice, thanks to her new juicer. Angie was really surprised and thankful for someone finally putting her first.

"Thanks, Ms. Ella, for the brunch. I really needed that."

"Not a problem, cuz. You know I'd do anything for you," she said giving her big cousin a hug.

"Well, I'm glad you said that because I need a huge favor. I need a place to stay for a little while. I don't want to go home to Earl."

"No problem, Angie. Of course you can stay here. I have plenty of space....when are you talking about coming?"

"Tonight when I get off work."

"What time will that be because I will have to let you in."

"I get off at 11pm, is that ok?" I asked.

"Yeah that's fine. Just give me a call when you head this was. I sleep a lot harder these days and I may not hear you at the door."

"Ok, thanks again, Ella. Can I ask that you keep what happened last night just between us? I don't want the rest of the family all up in my business."

"They won't hear anything from me," Ella said agreeing that it was Angie's business, but she also knew that Angie would nut the hell up if she did say anything.

After Angie left for work, Ella went about her day as usual. Ella has been a full time college student for the past 5 months. She had the luxury of not having to work during her pregnancy because of a little slip of the tongue while working at the casino. Truth be told, Ella cursed out one of her employees and got fired. Normally, she was a happy, humorous person. But anyone who really knew her knew that there was a fine line between her being cool and a flat out nut. Let some family members tell it, she is crazy; but the truth is that Ella suffered from Post-Traumatic Stress Disorder (PTSD) due to some terrible things that occurred while she was in the military. The family doesn't really know much about her military time because she doesn't talk about it. They do know that when she is in one of her moods, it is in their best interest to just leave her alone.

After class, Ella went by her mom's house for her daily visit. She knew that she could not tell her mom about what happened to Angle last night because it would be all over the family by morning.

"Ella, did you leave the house early this morning?"

"Why you ask me that Ma?"

"Cause ya step daddy said he heard something

that sounded like a car door slamming around 2 something this morning."

"Ma, tell your husband to mind his business please. I mighta been creeping out to see a man," Ella joked.

They laughed it off, but Ella's mom, Elaine, knew that she was hiding something. By 7pm, Ella was dog tired and decided to head home for a nap. She quickly learned that being in her third trimester wiped out all of her energy. Knowing that Angie would be coming home around 11:30pm, Ella made sure that she was awake for her, but 11:30pm came and went. Around midnight, Ella got worried and decided to call Angie but got no answer. At 1am she tried to call her again, and by then she couldn't take it anymore. Ella went to sleep on the sofa so that she would be able to hear the door, just in case.

Angie never showed up or called and by the next day, Ella's name was mud! As usual, Ella wad-dled next door to her mom's for lunch and her dai-ly dose of gossip only to find that she was the topic.

"It's about damn time you got here girl," said an anxious Elaine as Ella walked in the front door the next afternoon.

"Hey Ma. What chu talking about now?"

"Why you didn't tell me that Earl jumped on

Angie the other night?"

Ella was stumped for words. *How in the world did she know?*

"Dang Mama, how do you know that?"

"Your Granny told me this morning over coffee. She said Mags called her last night and told her everything…said the fool hit the girl with an iron pipe!"

"Well, I guess it's out now and I'm off the hook," said Ella.

"And guess what else she told her?"

"What?"

"Angie told them that when she came to your house you wouldn't let her in. Said she banged and banged on the door but you never answered so she had no choice but to go back home to Earl."

"WHAT DA WHAT??? Ma, I did no sucha thing!" yelled Ella.

At this point, Ella decided to tell Elaine everything because right now she could not believe what she was hearing. After she selflessly got out of her bed in the wee hours of the morning and opened her home to Angie, why would she lie on her like that? They both knew this was all a lie because Elaine was Angie's aunt and she only lived next door. If she needed a place to go she could have went there too. All she needed was an excuse to go back…looks like Ella was it.

I Wanna Be Your Man

The day was starting off better than normal for Angie. She had a little pep in her step and was in a talkative mood. From months of working 6 days a week at the casino she was reaping the benefits of money well earned. It had been such a long time since she had made an honest living outside of doing hair and that wasn't too honest because she didn't have a license. The job was working out well and a promotion was in the near future. In the past she would only get a job if she needed extra money and then once she earned what she needed, she would quit. Not this time though, Angie liked working at the gift shop in the casino. It was open 18 hours a day, 7 days a week and there was plenty of time for her to get some overtime.

The house was quiet because she was alone again; Earl and Tesha were hunting and had

left before daybreak. Angie looked around trying to decide what she wanted to do first. It was
Memorial Day weekend and she was off, which
was rare, so she wanted to make the most of it. She
started cleaning her room first and then moved to
the living room and kitchen. Angie cleaned like she
had a new lease on life. The soft sounds of Luther
Vandross filled the background as she swept and
mop the floors. She sang along to Luther's rendi-
tion of Heatwave's *Always and Forever* as she made
her way to the other end of the house.

When she entered Tesha's room, the odor in
there made her face draw up. *Damn that girl is nasty.*
Angie went about picking up clothes off the floor
and making up her bed. After straightening out the
closet, she went over to the desk that sat in the corner. It was full of papers. Angie tried to stack the
loose papers neatly and organize the knick-knacks
when she ran across a letter addressed to Tesha. It
was already open, so she decided to read it. *Who is
Kalvin Henderson?* As Angie read, she surmised that
Kalvin must be Tesha's boyfriend and that he had to
be in the military because the letter was post marked
from an Army Base. *So Tesha's got a man. I wonder
what Earl gonna think about that. From the sounds of
it, they were real close, too.* Page two confirmed her
thoughts because he ended the letter saying that

he couldn't wait until he was insider her sweetness again. *I can't wait to see that SOB's face when he sees that his little sweet Tesha ain't his baby no more.*

※

Earl and Tesha came home with a doe on the back of the truck. Sometimes when they went hunting they actually killed something. Earl had bought her a rifle and was teaching her how to shoot, something Angie didn't even want to try. He liked hanging with Tesha because she was like one of the guys; nothing was like what they had. They walked in, Tesha behind Earl, both carrying their rifles by their side.

"Damn girl, what chu cooking?" asked Earl.

"Nothing much just some collards, fried chicken, potato salad, mac and cheese, string beans with potatoes and some peach cobbler," she said removing the cobbler from the oven.

"What's the occasion auntie?" Tesha asked taking off her hunting gear.

"Nothing special. My mama will be here in a few minutes," she said smiling while their smiles dropped.

It's not like they didn't like Mags, they did. It was just that they would have to be on their best behavior.

"How long is she gonna be here?" Earl asked.

"Just a few weeks; she came to see Granny."

Just then, there was a knock at the door. Mags walked in with a smile. After exchanging pleasantries, they all settled in for a nice family dinner.

"Baby, dinner was great. Who taught you how to cook like that?" Mags smiled.

"Mama, you know you taught me everything I know about cooking," Angie said clearing the dishes. She was still in a good mood; Earl and Tesha were confused because they didn't know what she was up to.

"Mama, did Tesha tell you her good news?" Angie asked serving cobbler and ice cream.

Tesha's mouth fell open slightly because she didn't know what Angie was talking about. Earl just sat there puffing on a Newport as if he was not listening, but his ears went up like a Doberman's.

"Naw, what news?"

"That she got a man in the Navy named Kalvin Henderson."

"Is that that boy Chell caught in your room?" Maggie asked between chews of cobbler.

Tesha's face fell to the floor. She had forgotten all about Kalvin and she didn't know that Mags even knew about that. Angie just smiled to herself as she watched Earl's face change colors.

"Auntie, where did you get that from? I ain't got no man," she said trying to laugh it off. She also saw the change in Earl's face.

"Well, I found a letter on your floor when I was cleaning your nasty ass room, and from what I read, it sounds like he is your man."

"Why were you in my room reading my mail?" she snapped.

"Because this is my got-damn house and I will read whatever the hell I want to!" Angie snapped back.

"Tesha, you better not have a man. You too young to date a Navy man," Earl said excusing himself from the table.

"But I don't have a man."

"Go get the letter," he demanded.

Mags felt the tension in the air, and she knew exactly what she was looking at -- a jealous lover. She didn't want to believe all the talk she was hearing from her friends about Earl and Tesha, but right now she had no choice but to think that they were right. It's bad enough that Angie insists on staying with his no-count ass knowing what kind of man he is, plus he used to date her sister.

Tesha came back with the letter and gave it to Earl so that he could read it. His face remained straight, but his eyes gave way to what he must have been feeling. When he finished reading the letter, his eye darted from person to person, and all eyes were on him.

Earl looked around the table and said, "Sounds like somethin' serious Tesh."

"Me and Kalvin used to hang out that's all," Tesha nervously replied.

"Earl, you look like you upset. The girl is damn near18 now, and she should have male friends. She can't be your little baby forever," Angie smirked. She knew this would strike a nerve with him, but she didn't care. He wouldn't dare say anything crazy in front of her mother.

"Na, na, nah, I ain't mad, just surprised. But if she gonna be screwing, she needs to be on the pill or something."

"That's a good idea, huh Mama?" Angie said looking from Mags to Earl, then back to Mags.

"I don't want to have anything to do with this, but Tesha if you are having sex you do need to be careful."

"Granny, I ain't having no sex!" she shouted.

"Gal, who you raising your voice at?" Angie asked moving closer to her.

"Nobody. I'm sorry Granny Mags."

"Ok baby, now on to something lighter; when are you two gonna make this legal?" she asked pointing to Earl and Angie.

"I don't know mama, that's up to Earl."

By now Earl was fixing him a drink to settle his nerves. His mind was racing. How could Tesha do this to him after all that he had done for her? *She ain't shit, just like her mama. Angie was right, maybe she is the only woman who's gonna be true to me. I can't believe this shit.*

"Well, Earl? When you gonna make my baby an honest woman?" asked Maggie.

"Whenever she want me to," he said to no one in particular, sipping his Paul.

Angie took this opportunity to go into her most dramatic performance yet.

"Earl...do you mean it? I want this so badly. We can go down to the court house right now if you mean it baby," she said hugging and kissing his face.

"I ain't going to no court house. If we gonna do it, we will do it right."

Tesha remained quiet. *He can't be for real about marring her.* She sat down by Earl and he moved, surprising them all. He was too through with her right now.

"Oh, Earl, I almost forgot. You got a letter too," Angie said shuffling through a stack of mail.

"I hope you didn't open it," he said.

"No, smart ass, I didn't open it. I signed for it though; it's from your lawyer."

He opened it and started to smile.

"What is it, Earl?"

"The lawyer said that I got a good case against the hospital from them breaking that needle off in my back when they did my surgery last year. The only problem is that I'm gonna have to let them take it out so that it won't move around."

After that slip and fall during the family reunion Earl had to have surgery to correct a slipped disk. When they were prepping him, the nurse hit a bone and broke a part of the needle off in his back. It has been giving him problems ever since. He ain't even supposed to be drinking because of his medication, but you can't tell him that. He hated having surgery because it left him in the bed for weeks. If it hadn't been for Angie taking care of him like she did, he didn't know what he would have done.

"Earl, when do you have to have the surgery?" Mags asked.

"It says here that I need to make the appointment soon so that they can settle this." He knew now that he was gonna need Angie more than ever.

"Earl, why don't we get married before your surgery?"

"Why? What's the rush?"

"Well, remember all the problems we had with your first surgery. I couldn't make any decisions for you. What if something happens? They know you're suing them. Something may happen, and I want to be there so they won't try nothing funny."

"I'll think about it, Angie," Earl said just before he gulped down his last swallow of Paul.

"Wait a minute, you just told my mama that you were ready whenever I wanted to, now I'm ready."

"Angie, can we discuss this later?"

"Now is as good a time as any. If you don't want to marry me then fine, but I refuse to stay here with you living in sin. If you can't make a decision right now, I'm going back to Bolingbrook with Mama."

He couldn't let her leave now with him having to have surgery again. Angie made sure that he didn't want for nothing. She even gave him sponge baths when he first got home. Tesha ass can go to hell.

"Baby, let's do it."

"You mean it this time?"

"Yeah, just tell me how much."

DILEMMA

*M*ARRIED…WHAT THE FUCK! Lord
knows I don't want to get married. Shit!
*What the fuck have I gotten myself into? I know that
I can't back out now; she will flip if I stand her up
again. This is all Tesha's damn fault. I got to get out of
this mess before it's too late.*

Earl sat under the tree outside just smoking,
drinking, and thinking of a way to get out of this
but keep his home. Everything was so good. Why
she would want to change it was beyond him. He
knew that he had to play along with Angie until he
figured out what to do. Deep down he didn't mind
being with her; it was just that he didn't want to
give up Tesha. Since he began teaching Tesha about
life, the other women didn't exist to him anymore.
He had given them up so that he could focus on
grooming Chell Jr. So why would he give all that
up just to turn around and get married to Angie? It

didn't make sense.

Women always want to get married. They think that a man will change once he says "I Do," but everybody knows that is a lie. Whatever a man is doing before the vows he will be doing after the vows, if not more. Marriage does not necessarily change a person for the better unless they want it to. Some women see marriage or a baby as the fix for preexisting problems in their relationship, but what they fail to realize or admit to themselves is that it is a cause for more problems if your shit ain't already right. You have to fix what is going wrong before lifelong commitments such as marriage or children are brought into the picture.

Days went by, and Tesha tried to talk to Earl several times, but he just ignored her. Angie was in hog heaven because she knew that her plan was a success. Earl walked around like he was just disgusted with Tesha all the while showing Angie more attention than ever. He and Angie went out more without Tesha; they even took a weekend trip to Destin, Florida, just to get away. Life was finally good again for them.

Earl was trying to make the best of things so he decided to throw some ribs on the grill. Angie walked out the door and yelled over to Earl, "I'm taking Tesha shopping with me. Here is your mail."

Tesha took him his mail, but he didn't even want to look at her. "Leave it on the table," he said over his shoulder.

Once they were gone, he sifted through the letters until one in a thick green envelope caught his attention. It was addressed to him, but it didn't have a return address or name on it. He shook it but heard nothing; it felt like there were cards in it, so he opened it. The cards turned out to be photos of him in Georgia doing a drug purchase. *Who in the hell sent this shit?* There was also a note inside:

> *You think you're so damn careful don't you?*
> *But as you can see, you fucked up.*
> *Don't be surprised if the police come knocking*
> *on you front door one day muthafucker!*

Earl looked around to see who was watching him. He threw the evidence into the fire next to him as he gathered the rest of the mail and went inside the house. Someone had been following him. The only people who knew about his runs to Atlanta were Angie and Tesha. He knew that neither one of them would talk. Earl also knew that if whoever took those photos wanted him locked up, they would have sent them to the police and not to him. Somebody is trying to scare him, but who? Earl was a real business man, ghetto hustler, but a business man all the same. He knew that he had to keep his friends close and his enemies closer. All his business partners had more to lose than he did, so he knew they weren't behind this. Angie and Tesha were the only ones who could cause him problems. Just then it hit him. He was going to marry Angie to keep her quiet because a wife could not testify against her husband. Tesha was gonna become his new best friend. Her mind was simple, and he knew that he could control it with the right words and benefits.

I'd Rather Be With You

*T*he wedding date was set for this fall, so there was a lot of work to do in the next six months. Earl wanted to hurry up and get it over with just in case his blackmailer started to make demands.

Angie was on a mission to make this the best wedding in town. On her paydays, her checks never made it to the bank. She went to every wedding vendor she could think of collecting cards and prices. She made sure that Tesha was with her so that she would know that Earl didn't want her anymore. Angie was the chosen one again. Every store they went to, Angie put on the biggest performance and made sure that everyone there knew that she was the bride to be. You know how salesmen can be; they gave her all the attention she could handle so that they could get her business. Tesha just sat back looking pitiful.

They went to David's Bridal for her dress. Angie needed a new dress because she burned the first one. She wanted all new things because she felt that all the items from her first attempt at marriage were cursed. With five months to go, the invitations were already sent, the cake was ordered, and the hall was rented. The only problem was the bride's maids. Angie had been so nasty to all her old friends that none of them wanted to be in her wedding. Naturally she was hurt, but she only had herself to blame.

Truth is she only had a handful of friends anyway. Most had known her through getting their hair done, and they just stuck around until she started to treat them like shit. Angie always had a good sense of humor; it's just that most times it was at the expense of others. When that expense started to get closer and closer to them, they pulled out. For instance, whenever one of her girlfriends would come over wearing a skirt, she would always lift it up saying, "Look, Earl, she got on granny panties." To her this was hilarious, but to the so-called friend, it was embarrassing. Earl didn't mind because half of her friends wanted him, and the other half he already had screwed, thanks to Angie. Some of these women were not offended and took Earl looking as a green light.

At least two of them, who shall remain nameless, slept with him behind her back. After they decided not to deal with her disrespect, they became hoes and tramps in her book, and she didn't mind sharing what she knew about them with others. Angie's biggest problem was putting others down to make herself feel better. Eventually, she convinced two of Earl's sisters and two of her cousins to be there on her special day.

A week after Earl received the first letter, he got another one, and this continued for the next few weeks. Each letter was the same but with different pictures all of him making drug sales or buys in different locations. He still didn't know who it was, but as long as the poe-poe didn't come to his door, he was not going to make a big deal about it. He didn't want to bother Angie with this. Plus, she was never there anyway.

One particular day, she left Tesha at home alone.

"Hey, Tesha. How you doing?" Earl asked.

Tesha was surprised by his question because he hadn't said a word to her in over 3 months. "I'm fine, Uncle Earl...you?"

"Good. Come sit down, I want to talk to you," he said motioning for her to sit next to him on the sofa.

"Look, I know that we haven't spoken in a while, and I want to say that I'm sorry. I was just so mad at you for being with another man. I had time to think about it, and I forgive you. I know that you didn't mean it and that you were just being young. It's okay, we all make mistakes. I want us to start fresh. Can we?"

Tesha sat there thinking for a second before she spoke. During the time that Earl had excused himself from her life, she started hanging out with the gay boy down the street. Mark was her best friend because they both knew each other's secrets and kept them. They had started to hang out a lot by going to the mall and to the movies both looking at men. But none of them were what she wanted because they were not Earl. She took a deep breath before she spoke.

"Answer one question for me Earl. Do you love her more than me?" Tesha asked wrenching her fingers together.

"Of course not," he said putting his hand on her knee.

"Then why are you doing this?"

"Sometimes we have to do things that we don't want to do. When you get older you will understand what I'm talking about."

"I'm almost grown, how much older do I need

to be to know that you don't just marry someone you don't love?" she asked folding her arms across her chest.

"Obviously not old enough because you don't know what you're talking about. People don't always marry for love, Tesha. Life can sometimes be complicated, and adults have to do certain thing in order to get by."

"I understand….I guess."

"So, can we start fresh?" he asked with sincere eyes.

"Yes, we can."

Earl wrapped his arms around Tesha and gave her a deep hug. In her ear, he whispered how much he missed her and loved her. Her heart was beating as fast as it could. She hated that she loved him so much. In the back of her mind she thought about what he had said about doing certain things to get by. That is exactly what she was going to do. Earl was her way to get by. She didn't have anybody looking out for her, and in a few months she would be legal and on her own. Now was the time to secure her future.

"Baby, I'm so glad that you forgive me. You know that I want to give you the world…and I will, but you have got to give me time, okay?"

"I know, Earl. I'm patient, and I will always be here for you."

The apartment was just like they had left it. Tesha had not set foot in their place since her secrets were exposed; it felt good to be home again. Earl had added some photos to the bare walls, so now the place had a more lived in appearance. They had the whole day to themselves. Angie was pulling a double at the casino because someone called out sick. Earl told her that he was going to Atlanta, and Tesha was supposed to be staying the night with Mark.

The two got comfortable. Tesha took a long bubble bath while Earl went to get dinner from the Chinese restaurant down the street, and the Paul was already in the freezer getting a chill. When he got back, Tesha was sitting on the sofa in just an oversized T-shirt and a pair of sexy red lace panties. Earl almost dropped the food that was in his hands. The years had been good to Tesha. She filled out in all the right places. Her breasts were a full "D" cup. She had an ass that would put J-Lo to shame. She stood about 5'6" with almond shaped eyes and sexy long bowed legs. She was Chell's twin.

"Did you get my egg rolls?" she asked flipping through the TV channels.

"Yeah, I got them. Ooh baby girl look good enough to eat."

She smiled at him, "Maybe later."

After dinner, they retired to the bedroom. Earl turned the radio on to the Quiet Storm and lit some candles. Over the years Earl had taught Tesha just what he liked in the bedroom.

Tesha began her slow wind to R. Kelly's remix of *Bump n Grind*. He loved to have a woman dance for him and treat him like a king. He had taken her to some of the local strip clubs in Atlanta where he knew the guy at the door that would let he in without having to show ID. He took her there so that she could learn how to dance for him. It worked, too. Tesha had become one of the best lap dancers that he ever had the pleasure of sitting for. It was like being in a Champaign room.

Earl watched her turn and bounce her ample behind to the beat. While he watched, he undressed and lay back on the bed with a smile. Tesha was slowly undressing herself with her back to him. She didn't really like dancing for him all the time, but it was all a part of her plan. She pulled the T-shirt over her head and made her booty clap…she knew this would drive him wild. Earl told her to come to him. Tesha cat walked in the bed and positioned herself between his legs. She massaged his legs from his calf to his thigh. She reached on the nightstand for the fruity lubrication gel that she had bought from the sex store and proceeded to rub his semi-erect member. The more she rubbed the warmer the gel became and the harder Earl got. He loved the way her hands felt on his dick.

Tesha bent down and blew on him; this made the gel warmer. After repositioning herself on the side of him, she took him into her mouth with one gulp. Her head bobbed up and down in his hands as he rested them on the back of her head. Earl's eyes almost rolled in the back of his head as she deep throated him. He couldn't take no more, so he pulled her off of him.

He flipped her on her back and started kissing her passionately; he could taste the strawberry gel on her tongue. While they kissed, she squirted some gel on her fingers and began to massaged herself. Earl kissed her down her neck and across her titties, taking one at a time in his mouth and showing it special attention. He lowered his head and gave her the same satisfaction that she had given him. Earl knew how to work a clit. Each flick of his tongue was met with soft pants from Tesha's lips. He sat back on his knees and grabbed Tesha behind her legs. With one quick motion he snatched her up to him.

He entered her with the gentleness of a first time lover. She was warm and very wet; he pulled back out not wanting to rush it. He entered her again and began moving slowly and tenderly while looking deeply into her eyes. They kissed, and their bodies remained in close contact. This was not just fucking to Earl -- they were making love, and both of them knew it. They both were too far gone to think straight. The moment he felt her tightening her walls around him, he knew that she was about to explode, so he pulled out and started sucking her clit with such force that her moans were caught in her throat. Once she climaxed, he entered her again and pounded her until he was spent. They lay there wrapped in each other's arms until the sun of a new day peaked through the curtains.

CONGRATULATIONS

*T*oday was the big day. The church was beautiful. Angie didn't use her home church because it was not big enough for all her guests, so she opted for the Mt. Carmel. This church had cathedral ceilings with stained glass windows depicting different scenes from the Bible. The pews were decorated with white bows, and the place smelled like a botanical garden because there were dozens of flowers everywhere. Angie didn't hire a decorator; she did it all with a little help from the family.

The service began with a solo from one of the ladies from the church. When Angie took a peak out into the sanctuary, she was surprised by how many guests had actually shown up. She knew that most of them were not even invited and that they had only come to be nosy, but who cared? They would finally see that Earl really loved her. This time Angie made sure that he was at the church with her. She drove him there and told him to get dressed with the groom's men in the children's Sunday school classroom while she got dressed in the fellowship hall. Despite Angie being disliked by more than half the people in attendance, there were still smiles and wet eyes filling the room. Everyone in the church, the minister included, knew the history between Angie, Earl, and Tesha. They were too surprised to see Tesha as a brides-maid. She did not look happy. Angie purposely made Tesha the last bridesmaid to come out, and as soon as she did, there were murmurs floating through the church. When the minister asked if anyone felt that these two should not be joined to-gether, speak now or forever hold their peace all eyes in the church fell upon Tesha.

There were a few people there who did wish Angie the best. They knew the situation was all messed up, but if she was happy, they were too. She had family from as far as Connecticut to come down for her big day. Chell, her husband, her two boys, and Mags had driven down from Bolingbrook. Three of Angie's cousins, Ella includ-ed, sat in the second row with their shoes kicked off just in case something popped off. They had made up in their minds that if Tesha so much as opened her mouth to stop this wedding, they were gonna kick her ass and Earl's too. If Angie wants to marry this fool, then so be it. But Tesha needed her ass whooped, and Earl needed to go to jail for what they were doing. But to everyone's surprise, no one interrupted the nuptials, and the wedding went over without a hitch.

The reception hall was decked out in tangerine, white, and silver. Everything was done really pretty. The table cloths were a burnt orange with white flowers for the center piece. Angie insisted on an autumn theme because it was October, her birth month. The wedding cake had four tiers in the shape of hearts with orange, silver, white, and yellow flowers flowing down one side. The groom's cake was in the shape of a large chocolate doughnut with strawberries filling the center. There were balloons in every corner and party favors on every table. The food was in buffet style with servers standing by.

Once the wedding party was announced everyone scattered to mingle and have a good time. There were unclaimed children running around playing with the decorations that Angie carefully placed around the room. The beer keg was popped, the bar was opened, and within the hour everyone was eating and drinking. Before dinner was over folks had started to notice that one thing was missing…

the groom. Earl was not in the reception hall. No one wanted to ask Angie where he was at because Tesha was also missing. There were so many people there that many of them spilled out into the parking lot with the smokers. Earl was outside standing in a circle smoking with Tesha and her friend Mark. Mags had to go get him for the cutting of the cakes. But no sooner than they smashed cake into each other's face, he went to the bathroom and was gone again. The look on Angie's face told most that she was not happy. She tried to put on a smile to save face, but people saw straight through that.

Uncle C.J. had just finished two-stepping with Ella on the dance floor when he decided to step outside for a smoke. As he rounded the corner of the reception hall, he heard voices, so he stopped to listen -- it was Earl and Tesha. He couldn't make out what they were saying, but he could see that she was sitting on his lap in the side door of Angie's van. C.J. had heard the rumors but until now didn't want to get involved.

"Tesha! Get your ass off his lap!" he snapped when he rounded the corner. "You two need to be ashamed of yourselves. Earl, this is your wedding day, and you got the nerve to be having this gal on your lap. How can you be so damn disrespectful? And Tesha you need to get your fast ass back inside and act like you know better."

She had already jumped up when she saw him. Tesha left Earl and went inside to sit down, but she was not happy about it.

Earl finished his smoke and went inside for his first dance with his new wife. Angie just looked at him and rolled her eyes. She knew that he was outside with her as soon as Tesha walked in and sat down. She couldn't even look at her. *This nigga gonna make me act a plum fool in here. How he gonna embarrass me like this? From here on out, I'm gonna make his life hell. I should turn those photos over to the police and get his ass locked up.*

"Smile, Angie!"

A flash of light brought her back to the present as the photographer snapped several pictures of her. Angie shook off her thoughts and grabbed herself a drink. She really wasn't a drinker, but tonight was the exception. She danced all night off that one drink.

The word of what happened outside slowly filled the reception hall because motor mouth Nay was also outside. She had just pulled up when Earl and Tesha walked outside. They didn't see her, so she cracked her window and lay back in her seat to listen. She heard Earl tell her to come sit on his lap, and when Tesha did, she heard them kissing. Nay couldn't believe her ears, so she pulled a compact from her purse and angled it so that she could see behind her. Yep, they were kissing like she was the wife. Nay shook her head because she told Angie that she should not marry that fool. Did she listen? NO! Angie held her head high and said, "I don't care if we are only married for one day, we're getting married." This sounded so stupid to Nay; she couldn't understand why Angie wanted to marry him so badly knowing what he was doing with her niece. On the surface Angie acted like she was in denial about those two, but she knew what was going on. Nay was the only person who knew for a fact that she knew.

By midnight the hall started to slim down with guests. It was time to call it a night. There was no limo waiting to take them off to their honeymoon. No hotel reservations. Just Earl's decked out Explorer waiting to take them back home to their trailer next door to the hole in the wall. The fairy tale was over.

CLEAN-UP WOMAN

The first day as Mr. and Mrs. was anything but typical. Early that next morning, everyone in the house was awakened by a blaring horn outside. Angie jumped up first closely followed by Earl; she was all ready to give some fool a piece of her mind. She opened the door to find an unknown truck sitting in their front yard. Once Earl saw who it was, he tried to get Angie back inside the house. Too late, she also saw who was driving. It was Meka, Earl's side piece from the PJ's. Earl had left that girl alone a few years back when she moved to Savannah so he didn't know why she was sitting up in his yard just as big and bold as shit.

Meka was a tiny woman about 4'11". She could not have weighed more than a buck 10 soaking wet. She was a nice cocoa brown with a short neatly cropped haircut the color of a cinnamon stick. She got out the truck and opened the back door. To both Angie's and Earl's surprise, two kids about 10 or so climbed from the back seat of the truck. Meka grabbed each by the hand and led them towards the house. The closer the children got, the more they resembled Earl. They had his lips and eyes. The little girl looked just like one of those Brats dolls that the little girls are going wild for. Earl and two of his brothers had the same facial characteristics; tight eyes, pointed nose, and full pouty lips. These two kids had the same features. Angie looked at Earl then back at Meka. It was clear why she was there, so Angie stepped to the side and let her in.

"How can I help you?" Angie asked offering Meka a seat, which she declined.

"I just wanted my children to meet their stepmother. Say hi to ya daddy's wife, kids" she said pushing the children over to Angie.

"Earl, what is she talking about?" Angie asked as the kids walked over to her.

"I don't know Angie. These kids ain't mine," he said stuttering.

Anyone with eyes could see that he was lying; those two looked just like Earl, and he knew it.

"Oh yeah, then what does this mean?" Meka asked handing Angie a manila envelope.

Earl tried to snatch the envelope before Angie

could touch it, but he was too far away. Angie pulled out the contents which were photos of Earl with the kids standing by his side. The letter inside was the results of a paternity test that said that Earl was 99.997 percent the father of Darrion and Karrion Jones. There was nothing he could say as Angie passed him the letter. Her face was flushed.

"So now what, Meka? You told on me. You ain't getting no more money from me, so I don't even know why you're here."

"I just thought that Angie should know what kind of man she is dealing with. Oh by the way, the child that I'm carrying now is also yours, so I will be seeing you two in court in about six months," she said looking at her watch as if it held a calendar instead of the time. *Earl cursed himself for fuckin with her just before he married Angie.*

"Well, Meka, I want to thank you for stopping by, but I think you should leave now so that I can talk to my husband," Angie said politely as she walked over and opened the front door.

Meka was shocked by her response because she was all ready for Angie to act a fool. She had brought her cousins with her just in case things got out of hand. Angie wasn't a fool. She saw those chicken heads in the truck when she first opened the door. Meka left without another word.

"You always said that you wanted a houseful of kids; guess you got your wish," Angie said as she closed the front door.

"Baby, I'm sorry."

"Earl, I thought you said that you were done with that bitch."

"I was…I mean I am."

"Then tell me why she was at my door step with your kids? I had heard that those twins looked like you, but I thought it was just talk…guess not, huh? What do you have to say for yourself now, stupid? I fucking hate you!" she said in a tone just above a whisper, but she knew that he heard her.

Earl had never heard Angie say that she hated him. She must have been mad as hell to say something like that to his face.

That damn Meka think she nickel slick. Her ass looked stupid when Angie didn't get ghetto on her ass; she should have though. I got the right mind to get my sister Tay-Tay to whoop that ass for tryna fuck my shit up. But I still got it, so I ain't even gonna trip. After she left I thought Angie was gonna start throwing my shit out…but I guess since she had an idea all along, it wasn't no big deal anymore.

Angie went back to her room and slammed the door. That's when Tesha emerged from her room in just a T-shirt and socks, wiping sleep from her eyes. She had already heard everything but was trying to play it off as if she just got up. She knew about the twins also but did care because Meka had always been cool as hell with her. As far as Tesha was concerned, that was good payback for Angie beating her, plus that would be less kids she would have to have for him.

Lately things have been back to normal. Me and Tesha are hanging tight again while Angie is working like a slave. She had done set up a bootleg beauty shop around on the side of the house. When she got everything she needed, thanks to me, she cut back to part time at the casino. I think it was just her way of keeping an eye on me.

I didn't mind giving Angie money because it kept her quiet. Tesha was just like her in that area because it kept her quiet, too. Just the other day I gave them both five hundred a piece to go shopping. One big difference in those two is their mindset when it comes to me. Angie will always bring me something back from the store, but Tesha, she only thinks of herself. Not one time has she ever bought me anything. I even asked her once if she had brought me anything back, and the heifer had the nerve to tell me "if you wanted something you would have given me some more money." I cut her ass off for a month behind that shit.

That mess with the kids worked out in the end. Meka let the kids come visit without any hassle. Once she saw that Angie wasn't gonna leave my ass, she just let it go. Plus, that baby she was carrying wasn't even mine, and I have the papers to prove that. To my surprise, Angie has been a good stepmother. She treats my kids like they her own. I know that it is only because she always wanted children. She also made sure that I set up a savings account in both their names and put them on my insurance. It's like she is a different person since we've been married. She started going to Mt. Carmel permanently and has even joined the choirs. Nowadays a whole week can go by without us really spending any time together. I didn't mind at first, but this is not like Angie. I can't help but wonder if she got somebody else.

No More Lies

One day Nay got the nerve to ask Angie about her relationship.

"Angie, I know you don't want to hear this, but I think that Earl is really messing with Tesha," she spat out.

"What makes you think that?" Angie quizzed never looking at Nay.

"Don't act like you don't see it. They always together, and don't tell me that it's because they just tight-like-dat. What father and daughter is so close that the child never leaves his side? Most children want their own friends. Tesha ain't got one good friend because she is up under his ass all the time. I know you see it. If it were anybody else, you would be the first to point it out and you know it," Nay snapped.

"I know" was all Angie could say.

"You know? So why do you put up with it?"

"Girl, this type of stuff been going on for years. Plus, he ain't doing nothing to her she ain't letting him do."

Nay could have been knocked over with a feather. "Angie, that don't make it right."

"Well, Nay, what do you suggest that I do?" Angie asked finally looking Nay eye to eye.

"Turn his trifling ass in!" Nay yelled.

"With what evidence, huh? I took her to a doctor a few years back, and they didn't find nothing. Now she is saying that nothing ever happened and so is he. So I'm just leaving it alone."

"Angie, it just ain't right."

"Nay if there ain't a complaint or some evidence the law is not going to get involved and you know that. I'm sick and tired of people trying to tell me what I should do with Tesha. Nobody was concerned when it happened to--…why is everybody so damn self-righteous and shit now. Ain't nobody tried to help me take care of her, not even her own mammy. I did the best that I could. That nigga gonna hang himself because if he get her pregnant, he's the one going to jail -- not me. And I'll be the first one in the court room."

Nay just looked at her because what she was saying was half way understandable. *If the girl ain't complaining and there is no evidence, what can the police really do? Tesha is loving every minute of being here with them. If Earl was mistreating her, you could never tell. Abused children don't want to be around their abuser, but Tesha makes it her business to be under Earl. Maybe Angie is right, he ain't doing nothing she don't want him to do. I hope she don't think I missed that slip of the tongue. I'll save that for another time. I am going to put some distance between us because this whole thing stinks to the high heavens.*

Nay just left it at that because she knew that nothing was going to change with them. But one thing was for sure, her daughters could never stay the night with Tesha again.

The Way I Feel
About Cha

Angie was caught in her own word after Nay left. She just sat staring at the TV, not watching or even listening. Nay's words lingered in her mind, but denial was always easier than admitting the truth. Visions of Earl a few weeks before the wedding came to life behind her eyes. They were lying in bed watching a late movie when he turned to her and said they needed to talk.

"Can't it wait until after the movie Earl?" Angie asked annoyed by the interruption.

"No, we need to get this done before we can move on."

He had her attention now. "What's up? Don't tell me you tryna to pull out."

"Well, that depends on you," said Earl.

"What do you mean? You do want to be with me don't you, Earl?"

"Yes I do, but this is not about you. It's about Tesha."

"What about her? After we get married, she is going back to her mama," Angie snapped.

"No she is not. I am only going to say this once. Angie, I will only marry you if you promise to never make her leave us again."

"What? I thought that this was going to be a new start for us…just us," she said tearing up.

"It will be, but if you send her away, you may as well go with her," said a very calm Earl.

"Earl, is it true? All the things people are saying behind my back about you two? Is that why you want her here?"

"Angie, I'm not even going to answer that. I want her to stay."

"So you are asking me to basically give you my niece."

"Well…yeah," he said in a matter-of-fact tone.

Was Angie hearing what she thought she was hearing? Had the love of her life given her an ultimatum? A trade-off of her niece for his hand in marriage?

"Now Angie I want you to think about this before you make a decision because what you decide will determine our future; it's all up to you. I will continue to take care of you just as long as you take care of me. Okay?"

Earl got up from their bed and Angie could hear him walking out the front door. He left her mind boggled as she just sat there rocking and gazing at the muted television. *Earl is not going to make a fool of me anymore. If he wants her, he can have her, but I will get mine. People are already talking about them, so it would be nothing new. His ass is about to get disability, and being his wife, I will always get my share. Payback is a bitch. When he has his surgery this time, his recovery will definitely not go as smoothly as before.*

HAPPY BIRTHDAY

*T*esha lay in her bed just staring at the ceiling. The sun was just coming up, and the sky had a deep yellow hue. She didn't want to get up and face the day yet. Today should have been joyous for her; instead, it felt no different than yesterday. It was August 23rd and now she was legal. Tesha had been waiting on her eighteenth birthday so that she could do what she wanted without anyone questioning her. She was still with Angie and Earl, but now she was an adult also. The set up was too sweet to leave, so for now that was not in her future. They didn't make her do anything she didn't want to do; she didn't even have to work anymore.

Most of her days were spent under the tree with Earl just drinking and smoking. No one bothered her and that included Angie. She hadn't talked to her mother since the wedding a few months back.

Ever since the incident in Bolingbrook with Enoch, her mother doesn't want to be bothered with her anymore. Having friends was still not an option because her attitude drove the girls to want to fight her, and she didn't waste her time with boys; at least this is what she told herself. The truth of the matter is that Earl kept her close to him at all times. He doesn't want her to have any friends other than him, and after what happed in Bolingbrook, she can't have any male friends except for Mark. And Earl only allowed her to hang out with Mark because, let Earl tell it, Mark had "suga in his shoes."

Tesha thought that having Earl was going to be the answer to all of her problems. But she was sadly mistaken when the fairytale did not come true. She can't do anything without him. Earl tells her how to dress because he buys her clothes; he even tells her who she can talk to and who she can't, family included. At first she thought this was cute because in her mind it showed that he cared for her and was looking out for her best interest. Now she feels like a prisoner. Earl still takes her on some of his drug runs to Atlanta and Miami. She used to love those trips, but they have gone from leisurely vacations to stop and drop missions. He doesn't even give her money like he used to because he said that she didn't know what to buy. Nowadays it was like pulling teeth to get a dollar from him. Being with Earl was slowly becoming more than she bargained for.

Tonight Earl's sisters wanted to take her out to a movie and dinner for her birthday, but Earl said that she could not go. When she had asked him for some money so that she could go to the Mall and buy herself something, he said for her to wait and he'll take her to the Mall tomorrow. The whole idea was for her to do something without him. *It's my birthday and I'll be damned if I'm gonna sit up in this house all night.* As soon as Earl fell into a drunken sleep, she took forty dollars out of his stash, something she had learned from her aunt, and tipped out the back door. When she got back from the movie all pleased with herself for making her own decision, she snuck back in through the back door and tipped to her room.

"Where you been bitch?" said a voice from the dark.

Tesha almost jumped through the wall. She cut on the light and was surprised to see Earl sitting on her bed. "I went to a movie," she said confidently.

"Didn't I tell you that you couldn't go?"

"Yeah but—" the smack across her face cut her words off before she could finish.

Earl grabbed her by her hair and bent her head

back so that she was face to face with him. "When I tell you not to go somewhere, that is exactly what the fuck I mean." With that, he pushed her onto the bed. Tesha just lay there holding her face and crying. This was not the first time and it surely wouldn't be the last time that Earl spoke to her with his fist.

Today was a new day. Tesha knew that she was wrong for disobeying Earl, and she knew that he didn't mean what he did last night. Tesha got up and went to the bathroom to take her shower. The hot water felt so good on her body. All the tension of the day before was washed away with each drop. As she dried herself off, she caught a glimpse of her face in the mirror. Her eyes must have been playing tricks on her because she could have sworn that she saw a dark spot on the left side of her face. After she dried the steam from the medicine cabinet mirror, she saw that her eyes were right. Right there on her face was a purplish bruise.

She knew that she had to hide this bruise. How could she face the day with last night's beat down speaking loud and clear? She threw on her robe and went in search of some make up. Earl didn't allow her to wear any, so she had no choice but to go to her aunt.

Tesha knocked on the door to make sure that no one was in there. She had heard them leave earlier so she should have been alone. When no one answered, she went into Angie's room and headed straight for her bathroom. Angie didn't wear much makeup, but on special occasions, she would get all dolled up. Tesha found what she was looking for and went back to her bathroom. She had no idea what she was doing, but the objective was to cover the mark, and that seemed easy enough. Once she started applying the foundation, she ran into a big problem; she was about two shades darker than Angie, and the powder was too light. She tried to think of a way to make it darker, but there was nothing for her to add to it, so she wiped it off and returned it back to Angie's medicine cabinet. Just then Angie and Earl walked through the front door with groceries in their hands.

"What are you doing in my room gal?" her aunt asked.

"Nothing. I needed a q-tip," she lied. She tried to angle her face away from them so that she would not have to explain the purple mark on her cheek. She was one step from her bedroom door when Angie called her to help them get the food out of the truck. Tesha snatched the bow off her hair and tried to cover her face with the loose hair and put on a ball cap to keep it in place. Once outside the wind caught her cap and took it across the yard. Just then Angie walked out the door on Tesha's left side getting a good look at her face.

"What happened to your face?" asked Angie.

"I…uh…I hit it," Tesha said trying to turn her head away from Angie's view.

"Yeah right. You must think I'm stupid. Earl hit you, didn't he?" she asked not missing a beat getting the groceries out the truck.

"How did you know?"

"Experience."

"What should I do?"

"I hope you get everything you deserve. I don't feel sorry for your stupid ass either. You wanted to be in my spot, so now you got it. You wanted to be grown and now that you are, I have nothing else to say."

Angie left Tesha outside trying to fix her face. She knew that the girl was in way over her head, but those are the choices she made. There was nothing she could do for her.

❈

Tesha walked over to Mark's house because she knew he would have something to cover her face with. He had been going to school for cosmetology and was pretty good at applying makeup.

"Girl, I don't know why you even bother with him," Mark said as he applied concealer to her face.

"I love him, Mark. When you fall in love, you'll understand."

"Ooh baby girl I understand that. What I don't get is why you let him beat cho ass," he said shaking his head side to side in that sista girl manner. "Now what you're telling me is that all the times I have had to patch you up was from him showing you love. Child please! I may not be in love, but I'll be dammed if I let a nigga kick my ass on a regular basis. What does Angie have to say about this?"

"She don't care. When she saw my face today all she said was that she hopes I get everything I deserve," Tesha spat in her best Angie impersonation.

"Well, do you blame her? You are sleeping with her husband."

"I'm not sleeping with her husband."

"Look…this is Mark you're talking to, no need to front…I know better."

Tesha refused to ever admit that she was sleeping with Earl. Earl was her man and not Angie's husband. They were just bonded by contract… not love. Mark continued to lecture as he fixed her face. She didn't like it when someone tried to tell her what to do, but she listened quietly to Mark because he was her only friend, and she didn't want to burn that bridge.

The Point of it All

*B*ack at the house Angie wanted to ask Earl about him hitting Tesha. She figured that this was the first time, and if Tesha stayed there, it wouldn't be the last time. Memories of how he used to hit on her came rushing back to her mind. Those times have been far and in between ever since they got married. Earl hasn't so much as rubbed Angie's back much less hit her. Tesha had taken her place with him.

After about a year of Earl and Angie dating, the abuse began. At first, it was just verbal. Earl used to put her down by calling her fat and saying that if she don't get her act together he would leave her. Earl made it his business to make her think that no one would ever want her because of the way she looked, and over the years she started to believe him. The brother was slick with his abuse, too. He never let anyone hear the awful things that he said to her. Earl never showed aggression in public; everything he did was behind closed doors. When the physical abuse started, he made sure not to hit her in the face. Since Angie was big, he used to give her body shots that could be easily covered.

In public he let her talk to him any way she wanted, but behind closed doors, it was a different story. To the outside it looked like Angie was wearing the pants in their relationship. She used to cuss him out in front of her family and friends, or she would talk to him like he was a child. All the while, Earl never said nothing, so folks thought that she was punking him. What they didn't know was that when they were home alone, Angie was a completely different person. She was the submissive one. She knew that Earl was not the crazy kind of nigga that would beat his woman just because the wind blew; he was more conniving. If he heard something out in the streets about Angie, good or bad, he made an issue of it when he got home just to keep her in line.

The opinions of others didn't really matter to him because he let her treat him so bad in public. What mattered to Earl was that he maintained control over her at home. Most times he ignored the things that she said to him because he knew it was all for show, but when he got fed up, he let her know by saying something like "all right Angie watch cha self." That would always stop her in her tracks because she knew that he only gave out one warning. Earl used abuse to keep the upper hand.

WHOOP, THERE IT IS!

*T*esha started getting sick right after the New Year. Since the weather had changed, it was easy to cover up her illness by saying that she had the flu. Nothing would stay down, so she stayed in the bathroom puking. Angie was a little suspicious until Earl started to get sick as well; she just figured it was some kind of stomach virus. She did her best to stay away from them so that she didn't catch it.

Thoughts of her situation raced through Tesha's mind as she walked over to Mark's house.

From the looks of things, I've gotten myself in a bit of a mess. How in the hell am I going to explain being pregnant? My aunt is going to kill me. What the hell was I thinking? Hopefully this baby will bring me and Earl closer together because I know that he really loves me. Like he said, the timing just isn't right. As soon as he gets his disability, me, him and the baby are blowing this camp. Aunt Angie can sit here and curse somebody else out.

"Mark, I'm pregnant." Tesha blurter out as soon as the door opened.

"A baby! What chu gonna do with a baby?" yelled Mark.

"Man, I don't know. How could I be so stupid?" Tesha cried.

They went to Mark's bedroom as they always did. Tesha had come over around 5pm when Mark got home from school. She didn't have anyone else she could tell of her situation, but she had to let it out before she burst.

"Mark, I can't take care of no baby. Damn, I just turned 18."

"Well, I'm sure I already know but, ahh…who the pappy?" quizzed Mark.

Tesha just looked at Mark. He knew it was Earl.

Tesha must have lost her damn mind. How in the hell did she let this get this far? I'm glad that I ain't never gonna be no baby daddy. Mark thought.

Mark shook his head and said, "So, what chu gonna do?"

"I don't know," Tesha stated rubbing her forehead.

"Well, how far along are you?" Mark asked rubbing her belly for emphasis.

"I don't know. But it has to be only a few months."

"Well, that doesn't give you a lot of time to make a decision."

"I know."

Lord what am I gonna do? This is all Earl's damn fault! It was his bright idea for me to stop taking my depo shots 'cause he said they were making me fat. Well, guess his plan backfired. From the looks of things, I'm gonna get real fat real soon.

CPSIA information can be obtained
at www.ICGtesting.com
Printed in the USA
LVHW011609230322
714164LV00008B/1875